Allen & Unwin's House of Books aims to bring
Australia's cultural and literary heritage to a
broad audience by creating affordable print and
ebook editions of the nation's most significant
and enduring writers and their work. The fiction,
non-fiction, plays and poetry of generations of
Australian writers that were published before the
advent of ebooks will now be available to new
readers, alongside a selection of more recently
published books that had fallen out of circulation.

The House of Books is an eloquent collection
of Australia's finest literary achievements.

A&U HOUSE *of* BOOKS

KENNETH COOK

Wanted Dead

This edition published by Allen & Unwin House of Books in 2012
First published by Horwitz Publications in 1963

Allen & Unwin
Sydney, Melbourne, Auckland, London

83 Alexander Street
Crows Nest NSW 2065
Australia
Phone: (61 2) 8425 0100
Email: info@allenandunwin.com
Web: www.allenandunwin.com

Cataloguing-in-Publication details are available
from the National Library of Australia
www.trove.nla.gov.au

ISBN 978 1 74331 567 5 (pbk)
ISBN 978 1 74343 296 9 (ebook)

Kenneth Cook was born in Sydney in 1929. He achieved recognition as a fiction writer with the publication of his first novel, *Wake in Fright*, in 1961. Critically acclaimed, it has been translated into several languages and is still in print today. It was made into a classic Australian film in 1971.

Wake in Fright was followed by over twenty fiction and non-fiction books, including *Eliza Frazer*, *Bloodhouse*, *Tuna* and *Pig*. His antiwar beliefs were reflected in his powerful novel *The Wine of God's Anger* and in the play *Stockade*. Kenneth Cook died of a heart attack in 1987 while on a publicity tour promoting *Wombat Revenge*, the second volume in his bestselling trilogy of humorous short stories.

Wanted Dead

CHAPTER ONE

"SO YOU'RE THE MAN I'm supposed to enrol as another of these bloody Special Constables, are you?" said the sub-inspector.

Riley wondered whether or not that was a question that required answering, decided it wasn't, and just stood where he was, trying to adopt an assenting expression.

"I asked you a question," said the sub-inspector sharply.

Wrong again, reflected Riley. "Yes, sir."

The sub-inspector leaned back in his chair and brushed irritably at a fly hovering around his face.

"Do you know how many specials we've buried in the past year?" he asked.

"No, sir," said Riley promptly.

"Seven," said the sub-inspector with relish. "We've buried seven. And do you know how many we've employed?"

"No, sir," said Riley.

"Seven."

The sub-inspector leaned over his desk and stared at Riley expectantly.

He has eyes just like a pig I once knew, thought Riley irrelevantly, again not knowing what reaction was expected from him.

"And that's only in the Goulburn district," continued the sub-inspector. "They die even faster around Forbes. to say nothing of Queensland."

Again he looked at Riley expectantly.

What does he want me to do? wondered Riley. Groan and fall to the floor in a dead faint?

"I suppose you think a bushranger is a rabbit, do you, that you can go out and shoot at your leisure?"

How did this man become a trooper officer, wondered Riley. Perhaps he was joining the wrong side? The bushrangers could hardly be more unattractive.

"Eh?" grunted the sub-inspector. "Do you think that—do you? You'd better learn to answer questions more promptly than that my man."

"No, sir," said Riley.

"And there's something I want you to know," said the sub-inspector, leaning back in his chair again and thrusting one thumb inside his shoulder strap. "I wouldn't have a Special in my division for an extra five hundred pounds a year if it was up to me. The only thing that makes it bearable is that you all get shot almost as soon as we take you on."

Most encouraging, thought Riley, something to look back to for comfort in the long nights ahead.

"No, sir," he said.

The sub-inspector glared at him in silence for a moment. "All right," he said at last. "The matter's out of my hands. Since I've got to employ you I'd better get some details from you." He pulled a printed form from a drawer in his desk.

"I have actually been employed," said Riley. "The Headquarters Division Commandant, Captain McLerie, told me to report here for my equipment."

The sub-inspector twisted his face into what Riley thought was going to be a vicious smile, but which turned into a snarl.

"When I want your advice I'll ask for it," he said. "And while you're under my command you'll go through the proper forms no matter what Captain McLerie might have said to you at some bloody drunken party in Sydney. Stopping bushrangers is our work here, not finding jobs for any fool of a jimygrant* who thinks he can do ours better than we can."

"Yes, sir," said Riley.

"Now," said the sub-inspector, spreading the form out on the desk in front of him and dipping a pen in the ink, "Your full name?"

"Dermot Riley."

"Year of birth?"

"The fifth of May, eighteen thirty-eight."

"That makes you twenty-seven now, eh?" said the sub-inspector.

"Yes, sir," said Riley.

The sub-inspector laughed. A most unmirthful sound, thought Riley.

"Do you want to know why I think that's funny?"

Riley hesitated between answering 'yes, sir,' and 'no, sir,' then decided on: "If you wish to tell me, sir."

"Because the last three specials were twenty-seven when I took 'em," said the sub-inspector. "And that's the age that's written on their tombstones."

He laughed loudly then, his eyes closed and his head back and his mouth open.

If that pig I knew had laughed he would have looked like that, thought Riley.

"Anyhow, let's get on with it," said the sub-inspector: "Height?"

"Six feet," said Riley.

"Weight?"

"Eleven and a half stone."

"Chest measurement?"

* Immigrant.

11

"Thirty-eight inches."

"Where were you born?"

"Dublin."

"Bog trotter eh?" said the sub-inspector, as Riley had known he would: "What's your general health like?"

"Good."

"Well I don't think it will be for long," roared the sub-inspector, half choking himself with laughter so that the last few words were almost lost in his spluttering gurgles.

"Now," he went on at last. "Can you read and write and cipher?"

"Yes, sir," said Riley, noticing that when the sub-inspector wrote he let his tongue protrude slightly. It was covered with a thick yellow fuzz.

"How about character testimonials?" said the sub-inspector. "I don't suppose you've got any of those?"

"No, sir, Captain M'Lerie said . . ."

"I don't give a continental what Captain M'Lerie said," interrupted the sub-inspector. "I'm filling in this form, not him. Anyhow, we'll let it go."

He seemed to tire suddenly of the form filling, because he ran his eye down the rest of the list of questions, then drew a line through them and put his pen down.

"All right," he said, "My instructions are to give you a horse, a pack-horse, a pistol, a sword, ammunition, camping gear and four pounds a week payable at the end of each month. You'll have to report here for your money."

"Yes, sir."

"And I want some evidence that you've been in the bushranger country," said the sub-inspector: "I don't want you loafing around in the bush two miles out of town and coming in here every month for your pay."

"No, sir," said Riley, wondering what sort of evidence would be satisfactory — the occasional scalp perhaps?

"You will at all times preserve your *incongeeto*," said the sub-inspector. Speaking straight from the book now, thought Riley, after he'd puzzled out *'incongeeto'*.

"Except in the presence of those you have reason to believe are bushrangers whereupon you may reveal your indentity."

That would depend considerably upon the circumstances as far as he was concerned, thought Riley, but he said nothing.

"This does not apply in the case of persons proclaimed outlaws under the Felon's Proclamation Act," continued the sub-inspector, speaking in a ponderous monotone with his eyes half closed as if to concentrate on remembering the words: "Such persons may be shot on sight."

The sub-inspector opened his eyes again.

"The only proclaimed outlaws in this district at present are about half a dozen men in Hatton's gang. so you'd better be careful who you shoot."

"I will, sir," said Riley solemnly.

The sub-inspector lapsed completely back into his normal conversational manner.

"You know about James Hatton, I suppose?" he said, leaning forward on his desk again and cupping his chin in both hands so that his beard was pushed upwards, looking, Riley thought, like a particularly dishevelled bird's nest. What could still be seen of the sub-inspector's face might be fancifully taken for some exotic mottled egg on which a child had scribbled rude and improbable features.

"Vaguely, sir," said Riley.

"Did you know they called him the Hangman?"

"I had heard that, sir."

"Do you know why they call him the Hangman?" asked the sub-inspector taking his hands from his face and laying them palm downward on the desk so that he could lean yet further towards Riley.

"Not exactly, sir."

"Because he hangs people," said the sub-inspector. "He hangs people who annoy him. He's hanged three people to our knowledge so far and the last one was one of our Specials."

He stopped speaking and stared expectantly at Riley. There was a fleck of foam at the corner of his mouth and another about an inch directly below, clinging wetly to his beard.

Perhaps he was genuinely mad, Riley thought. The pause in the conversation seemed to go on indefinitely, but Riley couldn't think of any appropriate reply. Eventually the sub-inspector said: "Your main duty will be to capture or kill James Hatton."

Then he leaned back in his chair and laughed, loud and long.

When he recovered himself again he said: "All right. Get out of here. Collect your gear and get on out into the scrub. And don't forget you're responsible for your own gear, any losses are deducted from your pay."

"Yes, sir," said Riley. He turned and made for the door.

"And don't forget to preserve your *incongeeto*," the sub-inspector called after him.

"No, sir," Riley said.

14

But that was likely to prove difficult, Riley was thinking some three hours later, as he made his way out of Goulburn in the late afternoon sun.

He was riding a dispirited gelding of uncertain age. His saddle was standard police cavalry saddle. By his left knee hung a police issue carbine in a leather saddle holster. On his right hip was another leather holster containing a police issue pistol. Around his waist was a leather ammunition belt containing bullets, powder, cartridges and caps. From his left hip, supported by a shoulder strap—which combined with the ammunition belt to give him a singularly military appearance—hung in its scabbard a vast and unwieldy cavalry sword.

Behind him ambled the packhorse, laden with camping gear which was innocuous enough in itself but which proved on close inspection to be heavily sprinkled with Government stamps.

A group of small boys followed him to the outskirts of the town, disposed to mirth, but quelled by the fierce glances which Riley turned on them and the way he fingered the hilt of his sword.

It was the sword that distressed Riley most. A gold prospector or some such wanderer might, just conceivably, equip himself with antiquated police gear in the interests of economy. But no one except a trooper would be lunatic enough to take a cavalry sword into the bush.

As he progressed slowly along the dirt road past the last of the houses the rhythmic, penetrating buzzing beat of a million cicadas secreted among the leaves of the trees made Riley feel as though he was riding in a fog of sound.

Moreover it was hot, very hot. Too hot in fact. He

could feel the sweat running down his neck under the collar of his jacket.

"I think we might camp soon," he said to the gelding. Its head was down and its feet seemed to be dragging already.

Not exactly inspiring company, Riley thought.

He turned to look back along the dusty track and the hilt of his sword dug deeply into his stomach. As he readjusted the weapon he considered hurling it into the scrub, which was now thick by the side of the road. But then when he reported in for his pay at the end of the month he would have to account for it, and God alone knew what value the Government placed on such objects.

A pair of wallabies bolted across the road almost under the gelding's nose. Riley instinctively shortened rein and tightened his knees against the horse's sides to control the shying. But the gelding barely flicked an ear forward and didn't alter its pace.

Well at least he wasn't likely to break his neck on this horse, thought Riley, unless the damn thing went to sleep and fell over.

About a mile out of town he found a clearing with a small stream running through it and decided to make camp.

He hobbled the horses, although he doubted that they were likely to move from where they stood, set up his one man tent and lit a fire.

"I wish those damned cicadas would shut up," Riley said aloud. And suddenly they did, so that an unnatural quiet settled on the bush.

Riley, startled, listened to the silence for a moment, then shrugged and went about preparing his evening meal.

Tentatively he opened one of the tins supplied as part of his rations and poked a wondering finger into the contents. It seemed to be a mash of some sort of meat and bran. He poured it into a pan and set it across the fire.

There was a chance that he'd be able to supplement his diet with game anyway and with that in mind he might as well try his newly acquired weapons while there was still light enough.

The contents of the pan had begun to bubble and surge ominously and Riley took the pan off the fire and laid it on the grass to cool.

He took the pistol and loaded it with a ball, inserted the powder cartridge and put the cap in its place. He might as well travel with this and the carbine loaded in future, he thought, just in case he did meet a bushranger.

Picking up the tin he threw it about twenty feet away from the fire, in the opposite direction from the horses, then raised the pistol and sighted at it. At that distance the tin disappeared almost entirely behind the massive sight at the muzzle of the pistol and Riley cast about for some less ambitious target.

Deciding on a tree trunk about two feet wide some fifteen feet away, he cocked the pistol, aimed, and squeezed the trigger. The pistol shook under the force of the trigger mechanism being released and there was a sharp click as the hammer struck home, but no explosion.

Riley inserted another cap and tried again. The pistol went off but there was no indication of where the bullet sped. Riley went over and inspected the tree. Its bark seemed innocent of any wound. He reloaded and tried again, from ten feet, this time again he missed.

Riley looked at the weapon and shook his head. He reloaded, held the pistol no more than two feet from the tree trunk and fired. A great jagged scar appeared on the right side of the trunk.

"Oh well, effective for close quarters no doubt," said Riley, who was already falling into the bushman's habit of talking to himself.

He loaded the carbine and found he could hit the tree at thirty feet but the bullets seemed to veer to right or the left, or up and down, with no apparent reason and could only be relied upon to land within a foot of the point at which they were aimed.

"Oh, God help any bushrangers you meet, Dermot Riley," he murmured. "God help them indeed."

What was possibly more worrying, he reflected, as he picked up his pan and dug a spoon into the tacky mess the Government expected him to eat, any game he encountered would have to come within reach of his sword before it was likely to find its way into his cooking pot.

The cicadas started their ghastly din again, but soon it became dark and they fell silent.

Riley went to sleep in his tent and dreamed of the grey slate roofs of Dublin, wet with rain.

Dawn broke with a clatter of kookaburra calls and Riley crawled out of his tent and swore aggrievedly at the raucous birds perched on the branches, eyeing him sideways. Perhaps one of them might make a better breakfast than the Government rations? But then the chances of his being able to shoot one weren't high, so he let the idea go.

His horses were still in the clearing, more or less where he had left them. They were cropping the grass and neither raised its head as Riley called a greeting.

"Sociable," he grunted, pulled on his boots and went over to the stream to drink.

He glimpsed his own face reflected in the water and decided that his beard, which he liked to wear very short, was looking a little shaggy. Going back to his tent he rummaged around in his gear until he found the small pair of scissors he carried for the purpose. Using the stream as a mirror, he contrived to reduce his beard to what he hoped was its normal, rather jaunty, appearance.

He thought about breakfast but decided against it. He still had a little money left and preferred to buy a meal at some shanty along the road. He might also be able to buy some bird shot for the carbine. The weapon wasn't designed for it, but he could see no reason why it shouldn't be used to fire shot as well as it fired a bullet. It wouldn't be much use against bushrangers loaded with fine shot, but then it didn't seem that it would be much use against bushrangers anyway.

Good God, he thought, no wonder the mortality rate amongst special constables was so high with this sort of equipment. It was the regulation equipment issued to all the New South Wales troopers of course, but then their mortality rate was high, compared with the bushrangers'.

Nevertheless, Dermot Riley, he told himself as he saddled his horse, you will not become the eighth constable to die in the Goulburn district. If you should be so unfortunate as to be accosted by a bushranger, you will defeat him by the simple strata-gem of running away as fast as you can.

Not that that was likely to be particularly fast, he thought mournfully, as he mounted the gelding and dragged its head up away from the grass.

"Oh, Paddy Malone," sang Riley, as he rode slowly along the winding road in the crisp dawn air that so soon would become too hot for comfort. "Oh, Paddy Malone, will you ever go home. 'Twas the thief of an agent that caused you to roam . . ."

He was still singing when the horseman rode out of the scrub and pointed a pistol at his head.

"Bail up!"

Well now, how unlucky could a man be, thought Riley. The youth sitting on the horse blocking the road before him could have been no more than seven-teen years old. He had lank unkempt hair and yellow watery eyes. One side of his mouth seemed to have an uncontrollable tendency to rise up towards his nose, as though he were constantly in the progress of giving a mighty sniffle. But the pistol in his hand was aimed unwaveringly at Riley's head. It was the same cap and ball type as his own, observed Riley with some comfort, and tried to edge his horse back out of the two feet range at which he believed such weapons to be effective.

"Throw down your money," said the youth, who spoke in the harsh unlovely tones that Riley had al-ready come to identify as the Australian accent.

Riley sat on his horse looking steadily at the youth, unsure of what to do. He felt that he would probably be able to get away with swinging his horse around and fleeing, taking the very reasonable chance that the one shot in the pistol now pointed at him would miss.

But that would mean abandoning his pack horse, and God alone knew how many months' wages that would cost him. Besides, while he had no moral objection to running away from bushrangers as such, it galled him to think of running from this sallow youth, who, he noticed now, had very bad teeth.

"I said throw down your money or I'll put a bullet through your head," said the youth.

Of course, thought Riley, he could just give the youth his money, all thirty shillings of it, and go his way. It was hardly likely that the youth would want anything else that Riley possessed. But even that idea seemed intolerably irksome and Riley sighed as he realised that some curious conscience deep within himself was going to make him do something athletic and very possibly dangerous.

Slowly he passed his right hand across his body, grasped the hilt of the cavalry sword and very slowly began to draw it out.

"What the hell do you think you're doing?" said the youth uncertainly: "throw down your money and stop mucking about."

Wondering intently what it felt. like to be shot in the head, Riley continued to draw the sword. His hand was well over his own head before the weapon cleared the scabbard. Still slowly Riley turned the sword up until the point was raised to the sky.

"Now listen, my boy," he said slowly, his eyes staring gravely into the youth's. "Unless you put down that pistol of yours I'm going to split your head open right down to your neck."

The youth stared at him incredulously.

"I'll bloody well shoot you," he said angrily.

"Go on then," said Riley, very slowly and quietly

so that the youth had to strain to hear him. "But if you miss, or if you don't kill me, I'm going to smash this sword right down through that skull of yours so that your brains spill out all over the ground.

The youth edged his mount back a step.

"Put that thing down or I'll shoot," he said, but his mouth was loose on one side and the other seemed to have attached itself to the bottom of his nose as though in a sniffle perpetually suspended.

"You throw your money down quick," he said again, but now he was speaking in the sulky tones of a child whose friends are not playing the game according to the rules.

Riley sat quite still on his horse, the sword held high over his head. His arm was beginning to ache intolerably and although he suspected that this youth did not have the immense determination it needed to kill a man, he knew that panic could well make him pull the trigger—pull it before he had to admit to himself what he was doing.

The two of them sat their horses, staring into each other's faces. Riley was aware of that silence that becomes noticeable only when it is about to end, and suddenly the bush began to reverberate once more with the regular buzz of the cicadas.

How did they all know when to start at the same time wondered Riley unreasonably, then thrust the absurd thought aside as he strove to glare steadily at the youth.

The youth seemed to be trying to think of something to say now.

"I wonder how many times that gun of yours has misfired," said Riley quietly.

The youth extended the pistol further towards Riley and turned his head slightly to one side.

"You pull that trigger," said Riley, "and you've got just one chance in ten of not dying suddenly and messily the next moment."

He saw the youth's throat work convulsively.

"All right now," said Riley harshly, "I've had enough of this, put that gun down now before I count three or I'm going to cut you in half."

The youth's lower lip was protruding and Riley wondered that a mouth could be so mobile. Nevertheless he felt an uncontrolled shrinking in his own breast as though the flesh was trying to recoil from the crashing blow of a bullet.

"One," he said, very quietly.

He saw the youth's eyes waver irresolutely, looking into the scrub on either side as though hoping for help from there. He opened his mouth to speak again, but shut it abruptly and stared helplessly at Riley.

"Two," said Riley, feeling his arm was about to break. This was the dangerous moment. Unless the youth dropped the pistol now he would have to charge him. But it was all the same anyhow, because he couldn't hold the sword in the air for more than another five seconds.

"Damn you," spluttered the youth suddenly, and swung his horse around, lowering his pistol.

Gratefully Riley dropped the sword, urged his own horse forward, grabbed the youth by the collar and hauled him clear of his horse, letting him fall heavily to the ground.

Riley slid to the ground himself and took the youth's pistol before he could recover.

The youth sat up and looked sullenly at Riley.

"I suppose you're a bloody trap* are you?" he muttered.

"You just keep quiet my boy," said Riley. "You've done quite enough talking for today."

In fact Riley felt a certain affection for the unprepossessing youth, partly because he hadn't shot Riley and partly because, after all, this was Riley's first bushranger. A small one, no doubt, but a bushranger nonetheless.

I never thought you'd get this far in your profession, Dermot, my boy, he told himself.

He kept the pistol pointed at the youth's stomach and wondered what on earth he was going to do with him. He could take him back to Goulburn, but that would mean coming into contact again with the sub-inspector well before it was absolutely necessary. He could shoot him on the spot, but that seemed unduly harsh and in any case it was unlikely that he could hit him even at that range.

But then it would be an absolute anti-climax, after this singular victory, just to let him go.

A kookaburra landed on the branch of a tree some twenty feet away and began its insane cackle, audible even above the blare of the cicadas.

Riley raised the pistol and aimed at it. He didn't particularly want to kill the kookaburra, but then he didn't think it likely he would. He was mainly curious to see whether or not the pistol would have fired if the youth had pulled the trigger.

It went off with an immense explosion and the youth's horse went galloping wildly down the road, its reins flying. Riley's own horse went on unper-

* Trooper.

turbedly cropping the grass. The kookaburra didn't stir or falter in its song.

Riley took out his own pistol. He'd forgotten to load it that morning, but the youth didn't know that.

"Well now," said Riley to the youth who was staring up at him in that diffident and ingratiating manner in which one looks at a lunatic. "Well now, it was just as well you didn't pull that trigger, wasn't it?"

That was a fool of a thing to do, thought Riley. He could reasonably have taken the youth's horse as spoils of war if he hadn't scared it away. There was no hope of ever catching up with it on his own mount.

An empty pistol in either hand, Riley stood considering the youth, aware that he would soon have to make up his mind what to do with him. He couldn't stand there posturing all day.

Uneasily a thought began to stir in the recesses of his mind. He caught a glimpse of it and suppressed it hurriedly. But it came back, niggling away at him, tempting him, refusing not to be recognised. Riley had heard about the bushrangers' *telegraph* system whereby they paid, or frightened, a number of people in a district to relay messages of the movements of the police, or of gold shipments or other booty.

One of the methods in which this information was relayed was to leave messages at the bushrangers *plants*. These were caches of food, guns, ammunition, and sometimes even horses, which the bushrangers placed strategically over the countryside along their escape routes. The main hope of any ambitious trooper was to locate one of these escape routes, or even one of the *plants* and wait there until the bushranger eventually turned up. Of necessity quite a few of the bushrangers' *plants* were known, but only to the people they used as *telegrams,* and these were notoriously reluctant to talk to the police.

But this abject youth now sitting on the grass before him, thought Riley, might well be such a *telegram.* He might even be a minor member of one of the gangs.

And what is that to you, Dermot Riley? Give him a kick in the backside and ride away out of here; you don't want to know where any bushrangers are. But then it *would* be rather stimulating to report back to the sub-inspector that he had found a bushrangers' *plant* and that a force of well trained troopers might well make a capture, if they were patient.

But who the hell wanted to be stimulated by the sub-inspector?

Riley scratched his chin through his beard with the muzzle of one of the pistols. He saw the flare of hope in the youth's eyes, but ignored it.

In any case, he reasoned with himself, it wouldn't hurt to have the information, if it were available. He needn't make any use of it.

He looked at the youth a moment longer wondering about the best method of questioning him, then went across to his packhorse which was grazing a few feet away.

The youth made as though to scramble to his feet, but Riley waved the pistols at him and said: "Ah, Ah!" The youth relaxed again.

Riley took a length of tent rope from his gear, fashioned a rough noose in one end and dropped it over the youth's head.

"Up you get," said Riley, giving a light jerk on the rope.

The youth rose unsteadily to his feet.

"Just walk over under that tree," he said.

"Why?" said the youth.

"Never you mind, just do as you're told." Riley noticed the sword near his foot, and he put his own pistol back in its holster, stuck the other one in his belt, picked up the sword and gave the youth a slight dig in the buttocks with the point.

"Go on," he said. "Over under that tree."

The youth walked docilely ahead at the end of the rope.

"What are you going to do?" he said, worriedly, twisting his head around to look at Riley.

"I'm going to hang you," said Riley.

The youth stopped, turned, and stared at Riley in incredulous horror.

"But, but you can't!"

"Oh yes, I can," said Riley, digging him in the belly with the sword. "Get along with you now."

In the shade of the tree Riley reached up and tossed the end of the rope over a branch about eight feet from the ground.

He drew the rope tight and the youth, who was still staring at him disbelievingly, caught the noose in his hands just as it tightened on his neck.

"You . . . you can't hang me," he said.

"Can't I?" said Riley, "Do you know who I am?"

"No . . . no I don't."

"They call me James Hatton, Jimmy the Hangman to me friends, I believe."

"But it's not true," blurted the youth. "You're not Jimmy the Hangman."

"We'll see," said Riley, and hauled experimentally on the rope.

The youth gurgled horribly and clawed at the noose with his fingers.

"This isn't going to be a very efficient hanging, I'm afraid," said Riley. "I could dig something up with a horse I suppose, but you're only a little fellow so I'm just going to pull on this end until I get your feet off the ground, then let you strangle."

The youth's eyes had begun to glaze and his tongue was lolling out, although Riley had as yet put no great pressure on the noose.

"But if you take too long to die I'll tie this end to the packhorse and let him drag your head off," said Riley.

"Or," he said thoughtfully, raising the sword and laying the edge against the youth's throat, just above the clutching fingers on the noose. "I could saw into your throat with this, but it's pretty blunt."

The youth's eyes were bulging and his tongue was working convulsively around the outside of his mouth.

"Don't dribble so much," Riley said distastefully, drawing away a step. He waited a few seconds and then said: "Did you want to say any prayers? Be quick if you do."

He drew a little tighter on the rope and stood there with an air of slight reverence.

The youth made a feeble attempt to kick him which Riley discouraged by sawing the sword briskly across his throat. In fact it would take a week to break through the skin with this particular implement, thought Riley, although he had to admit it had come in surprisingly handy so far.

"Finished?" he asked.

The youth groaned.

"Well let's get on with it," said Riley, and then as though struck by an afterthought. "By the way, you know Jimmy the Hangman don't you?"

The youth shook his head. Then, as though he thought knowledge of Jimmy the Hangman might afford some protection, he nodded vigorously, then he changed his mind and shook his head again.

"I know you know him, or you wouldn't have known I wasn't him," said Riley, wondering whether so involved a sentence would be comprehensible to the youth in his present condition.

"Now I'll tell you what. You tell me where I can find him and I'll let you go."

"I don't know," blubbered the youth.

Riley hauled on the rope. The youth was standing on the tips of his toes now, his hands still clawing ineffectually at the noose around his neck.

"I wouldn't do that if I were you," said Riley, "it'll only take you longer to die that way."

He waited for a full half minute.

"I haven't got much more time to waste," he said. "Tell me where I might be able to find the Hangman and I'll let you go, otherwise I'm going to pull till your toes clear the ground."

"I swear to God I don't know," groaned the youth.

"Just tell me where I might find him. You know where his *plants* are don't you?"

He jerked on the rope. "Don't you?"

"Let me down," screamed the youth, "let me down for a minute and I'll talk to you."

"Don't you attempt to make bargains with me, young man," said Riley severely, giving another haul on the rope, but relaxing it again slightly because the youth's face suddenly went a vivid purple. "Just make up your mind whether you prefer to die or tell me what I want to know. It's all the same to me. Come on now. Where are Jimmy's *plants?*"

"I only know where one is. Only one."

"Well, where is it then? and I'll think about letting you go."

"Jimmy'd kill me if I told you," said the boy, who was so far gone in fear that he didn't notice that Riley had almost completely relaxed the pressure on the rope.

"I'll kill you if you don't," said Riley, reasonably, poking the point of the sword into the youth's throat, close up under his chin-bone.

"On the ridge above Lightning Fork," gasped the youth. "There's a cave there, that's one of his *plants*. It's the only one I know; I swear to God it is."

"And where exactly is this Lightning Fork?" asked Riley.

"About ten miles north along this road," said the youth, speaking nervously, but eagerly now, aware at last that he was no longer actually in the process of being hanged.

"And how do I recognise this Lightning Fork?" asked Riley.

"Why . . . it's where the Lightning Fork shanty is," said the youth, as though this was something everybody should know.

"And the ridge?"

"Well, there's only the one ridge, Mister," said the youth, in the same tone of voice.

"Sure you're telling me the truth," said Riley. "Because you're coming with me while I check and if you've been wasting my time I'll kill you."

"It's the truth, Mister, honest to God it is. I'll come with you, sure. It's the truth all right."

Riley studied the terrified, tear wet face and decided that it almost certainly was the truth.

He let go the end of the rope and the youth fell sobbing to the ground.

Riley delicately slipped the noose over his head and began to coil the rope.·

"All right, my boy," he said, "you can run along: but I'd give up bushranging if I were you; I don't think you're cut out for it."

The youth sank his head into the grass and sobbed.

Riley stood over him feeling a little ashamed of himself. He bent down and put a hand on the youth's shoulder: "Come on now," he said: "I didn't really hurt you, you know."

The youth's shoulders heaved and he pushed petulantly at the air with one hand. Riley was uncomfortably reminded of a fight he had once had at school, when his opponent, a big husky boy, had unaccountably crumpled and behaved much like this. And that had been long ago, far away, in a different, kinder land than this.

Riley slipped the sword back into its scabbard, climbed onto his horse, hauled its head up with the reins, plucked at the lead rope to enliven the packhorse and rode away along the road.

When Riley last saw the young bushranger he was sitting up, rubbing his eyes with his fists.

CHAPTER TWO

THERE WAS ABSOLUTELY no need to go anywhere near the supposed cave above Lightning Fork, Riley told himself as his little cavalcade moved along the road so slowly as to barely raise the dust. Absolutely no need at all. All that was required was that he should manage to survive as best he could in the bush until such time as he could go back to Goulburn and claim his month's wages. After that he should be able to manage quite comfortably, almost indefinitely. Or at least until the police force tired of paying him. Eventually, please God, something would turn up which would enable him to go back to Ireland . . . away from this slightly absurd, raw, new country. He only needed a couple of thousand pounds. A couple of thousand pounds would straighten out everything at home. Perhaps he should have gone gold prospecting instead of hunting, or rather avoiding, bushrangers. But then he knew less about gold prospecting than he knew about police work.

Anyhow, going near this plant above Lightning Fork couldn't possibly do anything to further his fortunes. Still it would be interesting to check on the youth's story by seeing whether there was a shanty at Lightning Fork, or whether there was a Lightning Fork at all. He could have a late breakfast cum lunch there and perhaps buy some birdshot. Which reminded him he might as well load his weapons in case he met any more bushrangers who couldn't be avoided.

This was obviously Lightning Fork, because the road split in two to make an island of a patch of scrub surrounding two huge boulders which the road builders had apparently thought it better to by-pass rather than remove, and in the centre of the island, growing up between the two boulders so that it looked as though it emerged from the solid rock, was the trunk of a vast gum, charred and split by a bolt of lightning.

Nestling against one of the boulders was the Lightning Fork shanty, a thatch roof building made up of slabs of timber standing upright, presumably nailed, or fastened in some way to a frame; a frame that had been made without great care judging from the wavering nature of the walls.

Riley looked around for a ridge that might possibly contain a cave. The road he was on ran through a slight valley in the tablelands. To the east the scrub rose and fell in gentle undulations until it merged with the heat haze in the distance. But in the west there reared a mighty ridge, a razor back, reaching perhaps eight hundred feet above the road and ending abruptly in a jagged cliff that brought the sky-line almost down to road level again.

Such a ridge might well contain a cave, pondered Riley. In fact if it did it would almost certainly be there towards the cliff where the top of the ridge seemed to be nothing but bare rock. Just as well he wasn't particularly interested, he thought, as he tied his horse to the verandah rail of the shanty. It would have been quite an arduous business climbing up there and poking around.

He went into the shanty confident that he could pose as an innocent traveller. He had no illusions about the sort of feeling people he'd be likely to meet would have towards the police, and his sword and carbine were safely rolled away in his camping gear. He'd hidden his pistol holster as well and his pistol, together with the one he'd taken from the bushranger, was tucked into his belt under his coat. He'd taken out the caps because he'd been rather afraid the weapons might go off of their own accord.

An immense, shaggy old man was leaning on the slab of wood that passed for a bar. He said nothing and made no movement when Riley walked in. The shanty was in deep gloom, or seemed so to Riley after the bright sunlight outside. Half a dozen barrels stood in one corner of the room with boxes near them, presumably to serve as tables and chairs. Another barrel stood on a bench beside the old man. It had a wet bag over it to cool the beer. Riley would have liked a glass of beer but he had already drunk the Colonial brew on the mistaken assumption that it would be much the same as the mildly stimulating drink he'd known at home, and he now knew better than to drink it on an empty stomach.

"Any chance of a bite to eat?" he said to the old man.

"Stew or cold mutton," said the old man in a voice that seemed to have a very harsh passage on its way out. Riley thought he detected the remnants of an Irish accent, but he couldn't be sure. The old man still hadn't stirred and there had been no visible movement when he spoke in the mess of grey, stained hair that hung around his mouth.

"I'll have mutton then, thanks," said Riley.

Staring straight ahead, out the door, the old man raised his voice.

"Dish o 'mutton," he called, and this time Riley thought perhaps he had a German accent. He still could see no movement in the man's lips; but then he couldn't see his lips for hair.

He heard faint noises of assent from behind the hessian curtain dividing the bar from some room out the back, presumably the kitchen.

Riley stood uncertainly where he was in the middle of the room. The old man still stared out the door. What an extraordinarily big man he was, thought Riley.

His shoulders seemed to be about four feet across. His head was crowned by a great thatch of grey-white hair that spread, at a roughly even length, down his cheeks and under his chin. A huge gnarled nose rose magnificently from the growth on his upper lip and his large, wide-set, staring eyes were almost hidden by his eyebrows. He was not unlike an English sheep dog, thought Riley; but what a magnificent build. He must have been really impressive when he was young, say about a hundred years ago.

"Nice day," said Riley, tentatively.

The old man said nothing.

Riley shrugged and walked across the room to the barrels and boxes. He selected the most stable looking of the boxes and sat down, quite slowly because he found the pistol barrels tended to dig uncomfortably into his lower abdomen if he moved suddenly.

He turned to the old man again.

"You wouldn't have any bird shot I could buy, would you?"

"Yairs," came the voice from the beard.

Riley wondered whether the old man was a dummy kept there as a front by whoever worked in the kitchen and given semblance of life by the art of ventriloquism. Or perhaps he wasn't a dummy as such, perhaps he had died some time ago; he looked so dried out and leathery that he probably wouldn't even have needed to be stuffed.

"Could I have a couple of pounds?" Riley asked politely.

"Girl'll get it for you. Ask her," said the voice from the beard.

There was no girl immediately in evidence, but Riley assumed she would eventually show up.

She appeared almost immediately from behind the hessian curtain bearing a tin plate of cold mutton and hot, boiled potatoes. Riley's first impression was that he'd met her before and he almost stood up to greet her. She was about eighteen, dressed in a skirt and high necked white blouse, quite a nice face with irregular features that all looked as though they might have been borrowed from different people. Riley guessed that the blood of several races ran through the girl's veins. But where had he seen her before? In fact he couldn't have. She must have simply borne some resemblance to someone he had known. He wondered whether she was the old man's daughter. She must have been born very late in his life if she were, but then he looked that sort of man.

She was studying him curiously as she laid down the plate and placed a knife and fork on either side.

"Did you want tea?" she asked and Riley recognised again the Australian accent, but it didn't sound so badly coming from her.

"Yes please," said Riley. "And, ah, the gentleman said you could let me have a couple of pounds of birdshot."

"All right," said the girl.

But she showed no inclination to go and get the shot. She stood by Riley's barrel and watched as he cut up his mutton.

"Jimmy Grant, aren't you?"

"Yes," said Riley, wishing she'd go away. Not that he was averse to attractive young women, but he didn't like being watched while he ate. It made him nervous.

"Been out long?"

"Six weeks."

"Good journey out?"

"Horrible."

"How long was the trip?"

"Five months."

"Not bad," said the girl: "It took you nine months to come out, didn't it Dad?"

"Yairs," came the voice of the old man.

"I came in a steamer," ventured Riley.

"I'd like to make a trip like that," said the girl. "I was born out here you see," she added unnecessarily.

Riley chewed away at his mutton.

"I'd better get your tea," said the girl.

"Thank you," said Riley, but she showed no immediate intention of moving.

A blow-fly made several determined efforts to land on Riley's plate. He waved it away irritably. The country seemed full of these noisome creatures, these and cicadas and kookaburras.

"What are you doing out here?" asked the girl with that direct frankness that Riley was finding as common in Australia as the blow-flies, cicadas and kookaburras.

"Looking for gold," he said promptly.

"Yes," said the girl, rather sadly Riley thought. "Everybody is."

She went away then and brought him his tea and a couple of pounds of birdshot wrapped up in newspaper.

"Staying around here long?" she asked.

"Don't really know," said Riley vaguely.

"There'll be a dance on here on Saturday night if you're still around this way."

"Oh," said Riley, interestedly he hoped. He didn't know whether he was receiving an invitation or just being given a piece of information. He finished his mutton and started on his potatoes, carefully cutting them into little squares.

"Going to settle down permanently out here?" she asked.

"No!" said Riley. "That is, I really don't know."

"I don't blame you," said the girl. "It's pretty dull."

She waited while Riley finished his potatoes and drank his tea, then charged him three and sixpence for the meal and the birdshot.

"I might see you on Saturday then?" she said as Riley left.

"Er, yes, I daresay," said Riley. The girl must see few strangers out here, he thought, in fact it would be a hell of a life for a young girl. She was rather nice too, with that long, black hair that a girl ought to have. But women were outside the scheme for the moment, he told himself as he mounted his horse and rode away from the shanty. Quite outside the scheme of things.

If he hadn't seen the path leading up to the ridge he would never have gone looking for the cave, Riley told himself irritably. But then if he hadn't been fool enough to go looking for the path he wouldn't have found that either. The trouble was that it had been obvious that if the bushrangers had a *plant* in a cave on the ridge there would be a path to it along which a horse could travel. No bushranger with any common sense at all would put himself in the position of ever having to leave his horse.

Then again it followed that if there were a path up to the ridge there must be another path down, because, again, no bushranger would have, as part of his escape route, a dead-end into the bush. At least it didn't seem likely.

The only point that was thoroughly difficult for Riley to understand was why he was now toiling up this path, leading his horse because the wretched animal seemed near exhaustion after travelling up hill for half an hour, and with the packhorse trailing behind.

Of course there was no danger in it, he told himself. If the place happened to be infested with bushrangers it was unlikely that they'd do more than take his money and that was hardly worth worrying about.

Unless they searched his gear and found the carbine and cavalry sword. That might upset them.

Anyhow, what did it matter? The odds were that there wasn't a bushranger within ten miles of the place and finding the *plant* could prove useful. He could use its existence as proof that he'd actually been bushranger hunting when he reported back to Goulburn at the end of the month.

The path led right to the top of the ridge, then ran along it towards the cliff. Riley found that he could now see the Lightning Fork shanty quite clearly and deduced from that that he and his horses, outlined against the sky, could be seen from the shanty and the road.

He led his horses quickly over the top of the ridge and took them a hundred yards or so down the other side into the trees, tied them up and walked back to the ridge.

He walked along below the path over the almost bare rock which would have been difficult for a horse but was quite easy for a man. It was late in the afternoon now and the sun was within an hour or so of setting in the western sky.

Just before it reached the edge of the cliff the path turned off the top of the ridge and led downwards on the opposite side of the road.

The trees were very sparse for about half a mile

down the slope and Riley could see the whole of the path quite clearly. There was no sign of a cave.

Now that was an extraordinary thing, he thought. He could have sworn the youth he'd terrorised to the point of collapse that morning had been telling the truth. The existence of the shanty and the ridge and the very path itself had all tended to confirm it. But there was no cave.

Of course there was no reason why the path should actually run to the cave. If it came to that, in fact it would be remarkable if it did. But if it didn't, how was he supposed to find it?

He began walking back beside the path, still keeping below the top of the ridge to avoid being outlined against the sky.

A ledge of rock jutting out several feet beyond the natural fall of the slope caught his attention and he scrambled down and found the mouth of a cave hidden below it.

The entrance itself was mostly covered by bushes and was quite small anyway. A man would have to crawl in on his hands and knees.

Riley stood contemplating the entrance.

If it were a *plant* it was an excellent and obvious one. The bushrangers could see the road quite clearly from here and would have at least an hour's warning of any pursuit.

Moreover, anybody following them closely, but not actually in sight, would assume they'd continued along the path and would never find the cave unless they came specifically looking for it, as Riley had done. Although on second thoughts, what would a fleeing bushranger do with his horse if he were trying to hide in this cave? He certainly couldn't get the horse in after him.

Then perhaps it wasn't a *plant*. Perhaps it was just a cave the youth had happened to know about and passed off to Riley as a *plant*.

That would have been a very reasonable thing to do, thought Riley, but then he wouldn't have thought the youth was in a very reasonable frame of mind when he was being questioned. And the whole thing hung together too well to have been concocted on the spur of the moment, under the peculiar circumstances prevailing. At least Riley would have thought so.

In any case the question of whether or not this cave was a bushranger's *plant* could be solved quite easily by going in and having a look.

Riley pursed his lips at the thought. Supposing there was a bushranger inside there now, armed, waiting and bloody-minded?

But there wasn't much point in reporting to the sub-inspector that he'd found a bushranger's *plant* and having a body of troopers sent out to find a cave that obviously had never been used by human beings. If it came to that there was no necessity to report anything to the sub-inspector anyway.

To hell with it, thought Riley. He might as well poke his head in and see what happened. At least his life as a special constable wasn't proving dull.

He thought about recapping his pistols, but decided that if there were somebody in the cave his greatest hope lay in trying to pass himself off as an innocent gold prospector looking for somewhere to camp the night.

That was the idea, he thought, taking comfort. He

could just wander into the cave, and if there was any-body there just wander out again, apologising.

Clearing his throat ostentatiously and shuffling his feet so as to give no impression of approaching by stealth, Riley went down on his hands and knees, pushed aside the bushes and went into the cave.

The cave widened abruptly inside and Riley was able to stand up in the gloom. It was dead quiet in there and Riley found himself holding his breath listening desperately in an attempt to hear the possible breathing of someone else someone else further back in the cave where the gloom became impenetrable.

But he could hear nothing and finally he let out his breath in a long deep sigh.

The cave had obviously been taken over for human use. Riley could see boxes against the wall and his feet crunched in the remains of a fire. It would be smokey in here with a fire, he thought vaguely. He looked more closely at the boxes and found many of them seemed to contain ammunition.

Riley struck a match and in the spluttering brief glare saw a few sacks half full and some more boxes further back in the cave. He walked a few steps deeper into the gloom which seemed to stretch a long way, but then his match went out and he made his way back to the pale glow of the entrance.

He didn't have enough matches to spend too many of them here and in any case he didn't want to stay inside the cave for long. It was reasonable to assume this was a bushranger *plant*, and so what?

Riley crawled out of the cave again and began to climb back up the slope towards the path. As he hauled himself onto the rock that jutted over the cave he found a large fissure running across the whole width of the rock about four feet from the end. He traced it round to either side and found it ran right down to the base of the rock. He broke a thin branch from a tree and probed into the crack. It seemed to be very deep, and must surely run near to the roof of the cave underneath. It was as though the rock hanging over the cave had subsided and cracked of its own weight.

Thoughtfully Riley stood on the edge of the rock over the cave and jumped up and down. The rock moved slightly.

Now that would be a most amusing situation, he thought. And it could be done—it could be done. But not tonight. It was too dark and would take too long. Briskly he set out to walk back to his horses.

The cave faced due east, and was flooded with light by the dawn. Riley prodded around among the boxes and bags fascinated by the trouble the bushrangers had taken to cater for every contingency. Here was tea, sugar, flour, whisky, blankets, bandages, salves, tinned foods, and many boxes of ammunition. The ammunition was of the type that contained bullet, charge and firing cap all together. It must be for breech loading rifles, and revolving rifles and revolvers that could fire several shots without reloading, Riley thought. Pity the police couldn't have these as well as the bushrangers. At least it would make the battle moderately even.

He searched through the boxes thoroughly, disturbing them as little as possible, but couldn't find any weapons. Which was a pity. A revolver, or better still a revolving rifle, would have considerably increased his confidence in himself as a special constable.

He probed further into the cave, which seemed to stretch a long way back. But he didn't go more than a hundred feet down because he wanted to stay where he could hear anybody approaching outside.

Taking out his knife he began rapidly prising the bullets out of the cartridges and emptying the powder onto a saddle cloth he'd brought with him. As he emptied the powder he placed the bullets back in the empty cartridges and sealed the edges down as best he could. It was a long job, but he didn't think it likely he'd be disturbed at that hour of the day. Anybody making use of the cave would be most likely to come there at night.

Nevertheless he tired of the work after an hour, when he had a huge pile of gun powder on the saddle cloth, and devoted himself instead to arranging the emptied cartridges at the top of the ammunition boxes, after taking out the remaining live cartridges and filling up the space with sand from the cave floor.

Then he packed everything back as near as he could to the way he'd found it, and crawled out of the cave with his saddle cloth wrapped around a great bulge of gun powder and cartridges.

He studied the countryside intently, but there was no sign of life apart from a wisp of smoke from the shanty far below on the road. There was little chance that he'd be seen from there unless he silhouetted himself against the sky-line. Making a rough funnel of one corner of the saddle bag he poured the gun powder and bullets into the crack in the rock, spreading the mixture evenly along the whole length of the crack. He made sure there was plenty of powder, even a slight overflow out the side, at one end of the crack, just where the rock met the earth.

Riley contemplated his work for a moment, then went back into the cave and brought out a few empty sacks he'd seen there. It was unlikely that the bushrangers would notice their disappearance, or would place any particular interpretation on it if they did. These he rammed deep into the crack on top of the explosives. The next hour he spent scraping up earth some distance from the cave, packing it in a sack, carrying it back to the rock and pouring it down the crack. Every time he poured a load in he carefully tamped it down with a stick, packing it as tightly as he could. He would have liked some clay, but there was none available, except possibly at greater effort than he was prepared to put in.

He didn't bring the earth right to the edge of the crack, but left the level about six inches down, so that a casual glance would not show that the crack had been filled up. A few strips of bark protected the powder he'd left overflowing on one side, and provided it didn't rain too hard, should have ensured that it wouldn't get wet.

Satisfied at last, Riley did what he could to remove the obvious traces of his presence and then walked back to his own camp, some two miles away, just below the top of the ridge where he could overlook the road and the path leading past the cave.

It was only when he arrived at his camp that he realised that if anybody visited the cave at night he wouldn't see them.

He thought about that for a while, decided that there was no way of overcoming it without undue risk and discomfort to himself, and applied himself to fashioning some fuses from gunpowder and the newspaper his birdshot had been wrapped in.

"There's no point in trying to plan this sort of operation too far," he told his pack-horse, "we'll just wait and see what happens." He was already beginning to regret all his activity that morning. It had seemed a good idea at the time, but now it was difficult to see that it had any practical application. But still, he had to do something while he was out in the bush, and all this would look good on his report.

But as Riley's days passed in peace he began to like the situation. It was not unlike fishing in a pleasant place without the right sort of bait. There was little hope of a fish, but the rigged tackle gave a sense of purpose to being there. He found that the birdshot worked quite well in his carbine, although rather less well in his pistols, and he was almost independent of his tinned police rations.

It was hot in the sun, but Riley's camp was among ferns on the bank of a mountain stream and he lay down and dozed around mid-day when he tired of poking around in the bush.

Three or four times a day, always at dawn and at sunset, he studied the road and the path to the cave. Several times he saw horsemen and buggies travelling along the road. Some stopped at the shanty, but none ever came up the path. Once he saw a coach drawn by four horses and escorted by half a dozen troopers.

He wasn't sure whether he'd been camped four or five days when, a couple of hours after dark, feeling restless because he'd spent most of the day dozing, he decided to take a prowl round the bush before turning in.

The sky was brilliant with stars, but there was no moon and the bush was a massive surge of blackness as it fell away below him. He could see a couple of yellow splashes far away which he knew to be Lightning Fork shanty. A little to the right he could see a flicker of yellow gold as though someone had lit a fire not far from the shanty.

The creatures of the bush were making noises all round him and in the branches of a tree above his head he could hear the harsh, asthmatic sound of a disturbed o'possum.

He glanced down the dark shadow of the ridge and felt an almost violent constriction in his chest because roughly where he supposed the cave to be was another flicker of yellow gold. Somebody was camped there.

"Well, now," he said softly to himself, "well now! What do you know about that."

He went back to his camp, loaded one of his pistols with birdshot and the other with ball, began to load the carbine with birdshot, but thought better of it, put it away and took out the cavalry sword.

After all, he thought, he'd only get one shot with the carbine which would probably miss anyway, and he could have as many whacks as he liked with the sword. Moreover, he'd developed a degree of affection for the sword after his encounter with the young bushranger.

He left the scabbard behind and carried the sword in his hand. The pistols he kept stuck in his belt, loaded except for the caps so that they couldn't go off. His newspaper and gunpowder fuses he carried in his ammunition belt with the remainder of his ammunition.

It took him half an hour to make his way through the scrub to the path, and then he cut back down on the western side of the ridge so that he could work his way back to the path again roughly where he judged the cave to be. There was too much danger of running into a sentry by sticking close to the path.

It was fairly easy going at first, because he didn't think it necessary to be particularly quiet.

But coming up the ridge towards the path he realised for the first time how difficult it was to move through the bush quietly in the dark. Stones seemed to be continually breaking away under his feet. The scrub crackled and rustled alarmingly no matter how carefully he pushed it aside. He seemed to be forever scaring up animals which fled with grunts, or squeaks or a scamper of feet and rapid, urgent shaking of bushes.

Every now and then he stopped and listened, but he could hear nothing.

About fifty yards from the top of the ridge, which he could now see outlined against the stars, he paused to consider exactly what he intended to do. He hoped he was going to reach the crest of the ridge just above the cave, but there was nothing to guarantee that he would. He had to reach the crest before he could orientate himself by the light of the fire. It was borne on him that his supposition that the fire was related to the cave wasn't necessarily sound. It was impossible to establish points with any exactitude in the dark, and the fire he had seen could in fact have been anywhere within half a mile of the cave. It might simply be the camp of some wandering prospector, or even a special constable like himself.

The only thing to do was get on to the crest of the ridge and have another look.

He went down on his hands and knees and began

to crawl slowly upwards, but found the sword was too much in the way in that posture. In fact a cavalry sword was a damned awkward thing to carry in any posture. He pondered for a moment, then slid the sword down the back of his neck, under his shirt, wincing as the cold metal touched his skin. He eased the blade under his belt and pushed it down a little further. That was better. He could move on his hands and knees quite easily with the sword like that. Moreover he could pull it out again quickly if he wanted it in a hurry. Perhaps he should include a recommendation that swords should always be worn like that when he put in his monthly report.

Then he discovered that the hilt banged the back of his neck when he raised his head to see where he was going: but it was still better than carrying the thing in his hand.

He found he could move very quietly if he felt with his fingers first and then slowly took his weight on one hand. He then raised one knee and moved it forward, lowering it gently to the ground, allowing no weight to fall on it until he was sure no twig or stone was going to move beneath it. It was slow, but very quiet. How quiet was borne on Riley when some coarse-furred animal, like a small bear, blundered into his face and then plunged away down the slope, grunting.

God alone knew what that was, thought Riley, grateful it was reasonable to assume that there were no dangerous animals in the Australian bush; or none that anyone knew of.

Then he began to think of snakes. Riley loathed snakes. He'd seen a few around his camp and had rigorously blown them to bits with his bird-shot loaded carbine. But now, here in the darkness, he might well place his bare hand, slowly and gently, fair on the coils of a black snake, or an adder, or a brown snake. Or one might strike him in the face as he painstakingly crawled towards the crest. That thought alone made him stand up abruptly, struggling to restrain himself from running up the slope to the clear rock crest.

Take it easy Dermot Riley, you're committed to this now. You're a fool to be here but you're here, so just take it quietly and go through with it.

He went down on his hands and knees again and slowly made his way towards the crest. Quite soon he reached bare rock and his progress became more rapid. Once he heard something slithering across the rock and he shuddered deeply, but the sound didn't come very near him.

He found he could move just as quietly standing upright on the rock, although occasionally his heels came down too heavily with an audible sound. He thought of taking his boots off, but the idea of stepping on a snake was too vivid in his mind and he decided against it. Besides, he didn't want to have to carry them. He left his sword down the back of his shirt; it was as convenient as anywhere.

He was very near the top of the ridge now so he took out his pistols, and, fumbling in the darkness, put the caps in. After that he carried them in his hands because he had no intention of shooting himself if humanly possible. Vaguely he worried because he couldn't remember which one was loaded with bird shot and which with ball.

A sudden clanking sound made him stop, and then he realised that he could hear voices. They seemed to be coming from his right, on the other side of the ridge. Very slowly, picking his way carefully over the rock, he walked to the top of the ridge, and found himself on the path.

The fire was about a hundred yards away on his right, down the slope, where the cave ought to be. Then he realised he could see the jutting rock outlined against the glow of the fire. The voices sounded louder now but he couldn't make out what they were saying. It was disconcerting to hear that they seemed to come from five or six different throats. He hadn't exactly calculated on battling an army.

All right, Dermot Riley, he told himself. You're here now, and what are you going to do? Well probably the first thing was to make absolutely sure he was stalking a party of bushrangers. It would hardly further his career if he entombed a party of perfectly innocent travellers in the cave. But that entailed going very much closer to the cave, and that possibly entailed being shot dead. But then he would have to go right up to the cave if he wanted to set his fuses. Pity he hadn't thought of that before he started all this nonsense.

He went down on his hands and knees again and crawled down the ridge away from the path and began to make his way towards the cave. Provided he didn't make any undue noise, he reflected, there was probably very little chance that he would be detected. Any sentries posted would certainly be on the path between the cave and the road. In any case it didn't seem that the bushrangers, or the inhabitants of the cave anyway, feared any attack or they wouldn't have had that fire going so obviously. Unless of course they felt that their numbers made them invulnerable. They probably did at that.

Riley's hand went down on some prickly growth and he chewed his lower lip in vexation as he wagged the hand in the air to ease the pain. Please God, he prayed, don't let me put my hand on a snake, because if I do I'll yell, and God help me then.

He settled down behind a rock about eighty feet from the cave and twenty feet below it. He had no intention of going any closer until he was reasonably satisfied that all the men he was stalking had gone to sleep. Cautiously raising his head above the level of the rock, he tried to catch what they were saying.

Only the odd word floated across to him, but one man with a deep voice seemed to be leading the conversation. Riley could see three men sitting around the fire and there appeared to be more inside, to whom the others occasionally spoke.

The deep voice was coming from a very big man who was sitting on his haunches on the opposite side of the fire from Riley. He had a vast black beard which spread out in a great fan across his chest.

They all seemed to be talking very quietly, as men do in the bush, and the few words Riley could catch were disconnected.

". . . on the plain country . . ."

". . . couldn't hit . . ."

". . . depends . . . on the hobbles, but . . ."

None of which was much use to Riley, but then he wasn't going any closer, not for the moment anyway.

But suddenly the big man stood up and said loudly and impatiently: "What the hell does it matter, we swing if they catch us anyway: A couple more won't hurt."

Well that was certainly prima facie evidence that this was a bushrangers' nest, thought Riley with satisfaction. Not that he'd had any doubt anyhow.

The big man said a few words Riley didn't catch, but then raising his voice angrily, he said: "If he does I'll damn well hang him myself," and stalked out of the firelight.

My God, thought Riley, that was Jimmy the Hangman himself, almost certainly. Of course, he remembered the police description: six foot three, heavily built, large dark beard, it was the Hangman all right.

Well now, wouldn't it be sport to bring in Jimmy the Hangman in his first weeks as a special constable? And wasn't there an enormous reward on the man's head? Did troopers get paid rewards? He'd better check on that, and, if not, resign before he brought Hatton in. What would the reward be? Quite possibly one or two thousand pounds.

And would you take blood money, Dermot Riley? he asked himself accusingly.

My colonial oath, he replied to himself, employing a phrase he'd heard often since his arrival in Australia.

Well now, Dermot Riley, it seems the only obstacle between you and fame, wealth and glory is to see whether or not you can in fact bring these rascals to heel. Why wouldn't they go to bed and let him get on with it?

Riley guessed he'd been behind the rock for more than an hour before he saw the Hangman and his two companions throw sand on the fire. From the noises that followed he assumed that they were crawling into the cave. God send they all went in, he prayed, because there was no way of telling now that the fire was out. Moreover it was going to be hard for him to find the rock overhanging the cave in the darkness. He'd better get moving soon or he'd lose all sense of its location.

But then similarly he'd better wait where he was for at least half an hour if he wanted his proposed victims to be asleep before he assaulted them.

There was nothing more for him to see, so he made himself as comfortable as he could behind his rock and contented himself with listening. He was gratified some twenty minutes later to hear the unmistakable sound of someone snoring very loudly. Surely everybody else in the cave must be asleep or they'd throw a bag over the head of anybody who snored as loudly as that.

His pistols became a problem again because he had to advance to the cave on his hands and knees. He could take the caps out, but then they would take time to reload, and he mightn't have time. Gingerly he slid them into his belt. No matter how he arranged them they seemed to point into his lower abdomen. He could put them in upside down, but then they'd point at his chest. Ah well, leave them as they were.

He checked in his ammunition belt for his fuses and matches and then began his approach to the cave. There was little scrub about and he was moving over almost bare rock. Provided he went very slowly, he didn't seem to make any noise at all. The trouble was he wasn't at all sure of his direction, within twenty feet or so. All he had to go by was the snoring and he couldn't locate that exactly.

Once his foot dislodged a small stone and it rolled across the rock with what seemed to Riley an anpalling clatter. The night remained quiet apart from the constant chirrup and squeak of insects and the snoring. A little later he heard a horse stamp and snort, but it was the peaceful relaxed sound of a horse settled down for the night. Riley wondered where the bushrangers had left their horses. The sound had seemed to come from some distance away, so there was little chance of his blundering in among them. He should have thought of that before. Horses would panic if a man crept up to them on his hands and knees at night.

He seemed to have been crawling forward for an hour, although it couldn't have been more than ten minutes, when he realised he could see the glow of embers from the fire. It was directly in his line of approach and it occurred to him that he'd been unconsciously heading for it all the time. That would have brought him right to the mouth of the cave and he didn't want to go there. He wanted to reach the point where he'd left the gunpowder overflowing from the crack in the rock, protected by the bark. Veering slightly to the right, up the slope, Riley crawled forward. He was breathing very heavily now, and, it seemed, very noisily. He tried to regulate his breathing into deep regular breaths, but found it almost impossible not to pant slightly.

Sweat was pouring down his arms and legs, but his body seemed to be dry. A sense of unreality began to settle on him and he was glad of the snoring because that gave strength in his mind to the idea that he was advancing on a party of armed and dangerous men.

Then, quite suddenly, he was against the jutting rock and had found the crack and the bark covering over the gunpowder. He leaned against the rock and tried to breathe quietly. Not that anybody in the cave would be likely to hear him over those thunderous snores, he thought, he hoped.

What would the Goulburn sub-inspector think of him now, he wondered. Probably that he was behaving in a singularly inefficient and dangerous manner. So he was too. Why? God alone knew. Anyhow, for Heaven's sake this was no time to be wondering why he was doing what he was doing. The idea was to do it.

He took out his fuses and wriggled them deep into the gunpowder. He wished he'd thought of bringing something to pack them in with. Earth would do, but he wasn't going to go scraping around in the dark for earth.

Another problem occurred to him. Once he lit the fuses he would have to get out of there suddenly. But if he made any noise some of the men might come out of the cave before the charge went off. As he remembered it the access from the cave to the path above was fairly smooth rock. The best plan would be to walk quickly up there and run down the path as quietly as he could. And God send there were no sentries. He didn't think there were.

In theory the blast should drop the slab of rock forward, blocking the cave, imprisoning the bush-rangers inside. If anybody happened to be directly under it they would be squashed, but so much the worse for them. They must have realised bushranging was a dangerous trade before they went into it.

But then supposing the charge wasn't effective and the rock didn't close off the cave? Well then he would just keep going up the path and lose himself in the darkness.

All right, every contingency covered, strike the match, light the fuse, and start moving. He took out his matches, breathed a vague and slightly absurd prayer for the general success of his action and . . .

Somebody walked quietly and swiftly across the rock not three feet from his face. Riley, kneeling, a match in one hand and the matchbox in the other, stayed exactly as he was, holding his breath, his heart thumping so hard it seemed something must give.

"Wake up down there, it's me!"

God in Heaven, it was a woman's voice.

He could see her skirts now, outlined against the stars and then she leaped lightly off the rock, breaking her fall by pivoting on one hand. Riley saw the hand, dully white on the rock, and then it disappeared.

The snoring in the cave broke and there was a confused murmur of voices.

"It's only me," said the woman, "Jane."

Now was the time, Riley thought quickly. Now was possibly the only time; light the fuses and run before the men came out of the cave. But dammit all, he couldn't blow a woman to kingdom come, and that's where she'd go if he lit those fuses. What the hell was she doing here anyway? Riley huddled against the rock.

He could hear somebody crawling out of the cave.

"Janey, is it? What are you doing up here this time of night, girl?"

"I wanted to see Johnny. Is Johnny here?"

A sudden flare of yellow light and the sound of tinder crackling. Somebody was stirring up the embers of the fire. The light fell on Riley's face and he could see the black outline of the man's head and shoulders. The man seemed to be bald.

"No, haven't seen Johnny for a while, week or more maybe."

"Has anybody seen him?" the woman sounded

worried. Riley had heard that voice before somewhere or something like it.

"Anybody seen Johnny Cabel lately?" the man asked in a slightly louder voice.

There were a few negative grunts from inside the cave. More men seemed to be coming out now.

"Keep your distance Jimmy Hatton," said the girl suddenly. "I've only come here to see Johnny." Well that was something, thought Riley. There was no doubt that Jimmy the Hangman was here. Much good may it do me, he thought bitterly.

"That's all right Jane, glad to see you for any reason." That was the singularly deep voice of Hatton himself.

"As long as it's only to look," said the girl, a little coyly, thought Riley. She probably was no better than she ought to be. And who was this Johnny? Her bushranger lover, he supposed.

The vast bulk of Hatton moved into Riley's range of vision and he could see the firelight glowing through the great fuzz of whiskers that flowed down on either side of the bushranger's face. Then he turned slightly and Riley could see his profile. He had a rather noble face, strong straight nose, deep set eyes, and a wide generous mouth. And this was Jimmy the Hangman, thought Riley.

"Well if you see him, tell him to come will you," said the girl. "Dad's worried about him."

Something in the way she said *Dad* caught at Riley's memory and then she too appeared at the extreme edge of the circle of light from the fire. It was the girl who'd served him in the shanty.

Then who was Johnny? Dad hadn't looked the type to worry about the prolonged absence of his daughter's lover. Perhaps it was her brother. Perhaps it was even that youth who'd tried to hold him up that second day out from Goulburn? Of course it was. That was why she'd seemed familiar to him when he first saw her, probably. And that was probably why no-one had seen him lately. He'd have been terrified of the Hangman finding out that he'd told Riley of the *plant*.

"You don't think the traps would have got him?" the girl was asking anxiously.

"No," said Hatton. "We'd have heard about it if they had. He's probably off somewhere with a girl. He'll turn up." Hatton had disappeared behind the ledge of rock now but his voice had a penetrating quality that made Riley shiver. It seemed that the man was speaking only two feet away.

"All right, well I'll be getting back," said the girl. There was a chorus of protest from the bushrangers.

"I'll walk back with you, Janey," said Hatton.

"Oh no you won't," said Jane quickly, and there was a burst of laughter.

"Come on Janey," said Hatton, "you know I've never hurt a woman yet."

"It's not being hurt that I'm afraid of," said Jane and again there was a laugh.

"All right, Jane," said Hatton, resignedly and Riley gathered that his approaches to Jane were something of a standing joke between them. "But if you get into trouble on the way back you'll be sorry."

"Much more likely to get into trouble if you're with me," said Jane pertly. Again the laughter.

"No you don't, James Hatton," cried the girl, "I'm off."

She appeared in the firelight, scrambling up onto

the ledge of rock. She turned round and slapped at someone behind her, then, laughing, stood upright on the rock, skipped a couple of paces to the left and jumped into Riley's chest.

She screamed, loudly and shrilly.

Riley stood up, knocking her over in a flurry of petticoats, and sprinted up the rock slope towards the path.

There was shouting behind him, and the girl still screaming. "Shoot that bastard," someone yelled. There was no shot. Riley stumbled and fell, scrambled up and ran on.

"Who is it?" "Shoot him!"

Then the shots. Loud crashing reports behind him and bullets cracking at the rocks around him.

Then the loud, regular bark of a revolving rifle. Bullets filling the night. But wilder now. Something struck his heel as though somebody had hit it with a hammer. He was limping, but he wasn't hurt. The heel of his boot had gone.

Footsteps thudding on the rocks behind him. Get off the path? Not yet. Keep running. Distance was the thing. Then the darkness of the scrub. He stumbled and fell again. Damn these pistols, and the awkward heavy sword. He'd kill himself at this rate. He dragged the pistols out of his belt. Which one had the birdshot? Damn it who cared? Someone was close behind him now. The shooting had stopped. They were afraid of hitting the man who was close to him.

"Stop you bastard!" A shot. He didn't hear the bullet. Another shot. Still no bullet. When was the next? It didn't come. The man's pistol was empty. Run. Keep running hard. Down into the scrub? Not yet. He might fall and then he'd be done. The bloody man was gaining on him.

Riley stopped in the path, turned, and fired at the black bulk of the man rushing toward him. The man kept coming. Riley fired with the other pistol. The man screamed and seemed to fall to his knees. Riley ran again along the path.

Now there were more footsteps. The others had gained on him because he'd stopped. Now they were shooting again. But surely they couldn't see him. They must be shooting along the path. Then get off the path.

He veered down the slope, stumbling and thrashing his arms, making for the belt of scrub that ran along below the rock line.

More shots. Near him again. They knew he was off the path. They must be shooting at the noise he was making. Slower, quietly. But you can't move quietly in the scrub. Then keep still. Stay where you are. More shots. What happened when a bullet hit you? If it killed you was there one flash of knowledge first, or did you just die? Keep still. Where were his pistols? They were gone. He must have dropped them. He wouldn't have had time to reload them anyway.

Voices. Boots on rock. They were coming down the slope. They knew he was here. But they couldn't. Not exactly. Keep still. Keep still.

Something was hurting his back. Good God, the sword! Thank God, he had something at any rate. But don't pull it out now. Keep still. They were closer. Another shot. The bullet was very near. They were coming right towards him. No good, they'll step on you. Bolt!

The crashing of the scrub as he ran brought the bullets. They couldn't be using the bullets he'd tampered with in the cave. They must have brought more with them. You can't keep running. They'll hear you all the time. You can't stop. They'll follow the noise to where it stopped.

God, but this stinking bush would be a rotten place to die in.

Get up a tree. There weren't any trees big enough. Get back onto the rock. They can't hear you so well there. But they're up there. They're all along the ridge. God how many of them were there?

Suddenly he was running clear on a strip of rock. Now he could hear clearly the bushes crashing behind him. Hell they were close. But they couldn't see him. What was that light? The fire. He was below the cave again.

Riley stood still, forcing his lungs to breathe slowly, so that he could hear. They were below him now. And behind. And God damn it, in front! There were men all round him. Of course, they knew this bush backwards. They were rounding him up like a chicken. Oh for a gun! To be able to fight. He remembered the sword and pulled it out.

Quietly Riley, quietly, if you're going to die, do it gracefully. There was another shot. But it was very wild. And several more. They were firing at something else. A wallaby in the scrub perhaps. Then they didn't know where he was, not exactly. But they must know they were all around him.

All right then, back up to the cave. Bending low he scrambled quickly up towards the glow of the fire. He knew what he intended to do, but not whether he could do it. If he could start a fuse alight, and then get up to the path before the explosion; they'd all surely come back to the cave and he could get out along the path, down the western side of the slope. Not the way he'd come.

Just a chance but better than blundering around in the dark until he ran into somebody. Almost in the circle of firelight now. Go around it. Keep low so you won't be outlined. Now across, over to the rock ledge.

No-one here; right, matches.

Oh God, that bloody girl! He'd forgotten her. There she was, just above him. Now if he went past her she'd scream and he'd be done.

Well damn the silly bitch, he thought ruthlessly, it's her risk. He struck the match and lit both fuses. Up across the rock now. The girl had heard him. She was looking uncertainly at him.

"Listen," he said urgently: "I've mined that cave and it's going to blow up. Get out of here."

He saw her mouth open to scream, so he slapped her face hard. The fuse must be almost down to the powder.

He grabbed her by the arm and dragged her after him. Surely she must scream now. She screamed.

Oh, God! What a mess.

The cave blew up. A sudden harsh glare of light and a dull loud crump. Then darkness, darker than before. Bits of stone flying around.

The girl was screaming.

Riley let her go and scrambled to the top of the ridge, then on to the path. There was shouting below him. And once the sound and flash of a gun. He couldn't tell where the cave was now. The explosion must have blown the fire out.

Run. Run down the path. But stay on the path. Remember the cliff at the end of the ridge.

The girl was still screaming. "Here he is! Here he

is!" she was screaming. That wasn't strictly accurate. He wasn't there. Not now.

What the hell was that? Hoofbeats. There was a horse galloping down the path. Surely no-one would be fool enough to gallop down here at night?

But someone was. Damn, but they must know this place well. All right, well he couldn't run from a horse. And he wasn't going back into the scrub again.

All right.

Riley crouched in the path with the sword hilt resting on the ground, the point upright. The horse was coming very fast—very sure footed in the darkness. Very close now. There was some movement ahead. The movement became a massive rush of blackness and the hoofbeats became enormously loud.

Riley leaped to his feet and yelled. The horse shied, reared, slithered almost over on its back. Someone cursed. A pistol fired. Riley moved alongside the horse's head and slashed at the rider with his sword. A hand grabbed the sword and Riley wrenched it clear and struck again.

"No!" someone said loudly, very close.

The hand grabbed the sword again. Riley pulled and the rider came with the sword, falling heavily off the horse. Riley now had the bridle in his left hand. The horse was plunging. The man on the ground was trying to get up. Riley hit him again with the sword, on the head, anywhere.

Then he scrambled onto the horse, but couldn't get into the saddle. It didn't matter, he was clinging on and the horse was away down the path. God send it kept to the path, he couldn't turn its head. God send it didn't just keep going over the cliff.

He could pull himself into the saddle if he let go

his sword. But he didn't want to let go the sword. Careful he didn't let it get between the horse legs.

Riley got a grip on the pommel and hauled himself into the saddle. He lay down low over the horse's neck and gathered in the reins. But he didn't try to slow the horse. It seemed to know where it was going and he was quite willing to go with it. There were possibly more horsemen following. But he could hear nothing except the clatter of his own mount's hooves and the rush of air past his head.

The horse swerved violently and then they were charging down the slope. So the horse was following the path. Not galloping over the cliff. Good.

Riley screwed his head round to look behind him. He saw a couple of flashes that could have been rifle fire, but no bullets came near. No danger from that. The greatest danger was that the horse would fall. And that danger was very great.

Again and again the beast stumbled, but with a scrambling clatter on the rocky path regained its stride. They were down in the scrub now and bushes on either side of the path whipped at his face. The horse's neck was warm and sweating. The smell was comforting. Riley kept his eyes shut and his head right down on the horse's neck. He daren't pull rein yet, not till the slope ended. Probably the horse wanted to slow down now as much as he wanted it to; but it couldn't. It wasn't so much galloping down the slope as falling in one long barely controlled tumble. Soon it would either reach the level ground or it would crash.

He still didn't have his feet in the stirrups and he didn't want them there now. This wild plunge down the path surely could end only one way and Riley wanted his feet clear. This sword was a bloody nuisance now. But hang on to it. You might still need it.

Then suddenly the horse was galloping across level ground. Riley sat up and reined in savagely. Reluctantly, its head unwillingly coming back, prancing and shying, the horse slowed to a trot, and then a walk; then it stopped, its sides heaving; the breath running loud through its nostrils.

Riley listened. There were no horses coming. He thought he could hear men shouting in the distance but the night was heavily overladen with the sounds of insects and he wasn't sure.

He relaxed the reins and the horse trotted forward again, purposefully. Presumably this clearing was part of the path, and the path should lead somewhere. Probably into another nest of bushrangers. But he couldn't go back. And he had no intention of leaving the horse and taking to the bush again. He'd never be able to find his own camp at night anyway. In fact he doubted whether he'd ever dare go back there again. Probably his best course was to try to get onto the road and ride to Goulburn and call out a force of troopers. Which, of course, was what he should have done in the first place, he thought ruefully.

The scrub closed round the clearing again, but the horse trotted surely forward and a path opened before them. Riley allowed the horse to take him where it would, only stopping every now and then to listen for the sounds of pursuit. There were none.

He had no idea how long he rode, blindly through the night, but dawn was breaking when he emerged from the bush onto a road. It was a comparatively well made road, and if he travelled south, it would almost certainly lead to Goulburn.

But on second thoughts Riley wasn't at all sure he wanted to go to Goulburn. He could with some truth report that he'd shot one bushranger and badly mauled another with a sword, but somehow he doubted that would impress the sub-inspector against the fact that he'd abandoned all his gear in the bush. Of course it would probably be there when he went back, when he dared go back. But what could he do in the meantime? He had no rations, no weapons. Even the little money he owned was stowed amongst his gear.

As the day grew brighter he tried to examine himself. His clothes seemed to be substantially torn to shreds. The heel was missing from one boot. His hands were badly scratched and so, he gathered, was his face. On the credit side he had a much better horse than when he started life as a special constable. This was a splendid beast, a huge bay of obviously fine breeding.

All right, so if he didn't go back to Goulburn, what did he do? He had no idea where he was. And even if he did, nothing would induce him to go back to his own camp until he was quite sure there wasn't a bushranger within ten miles of the ridge. He might be able to throw himself on the charity of some squatter, if he saw a homestead, but he hadn't heard that squatters were particularly charitable people.

Damn it Dermot Riley, why did you ever leave home? Come to that, he knew very well.

An insane cackle burst out of the bush on either side of the road and was taken up among the trees ahead of him. And those wretched things didn't make life any easier for him. Still, he thought wryly, it would all make a good story to tell sometime. He hadn't really come out of it all that badly.

The cries of the kookaburras must have cloaked the sound of the hoofbeats because Riley, without any warning, rode round a bend and found he was within a hundred yards of four troopers, cantering down the road towards him.

That at least solved the problem of what he was going to do. They would be bound to question him. But why on earth were they pulling their guns out? Certainly he still had his sword in one hand, but he couldn't have looked all that dangerous.

Eight hours later he was in the Goulburn Gaol charged with being in possession of a stolen horse, to wit Cicero, the finest race horse in the district, missing these three months from the property of Mr. C. Collingwood, grazier of Goulburn.

CHAPTER THREE

"THAT ALL SOUNDS VERY unlikely," said the sub-inspector, almost genially Riley observed with surprise.

"I appreciate that, sir," said Riley, "but it can all be checked to a degree if I could take a party of troopers up to the cave."

"To a degree, to a degree," said the sub-inspector. "A party of troopers will go to the cave, if it exists, but you won't take them. Oh no, you won't take them. You'll wait here in the cells until they report back."

"Well, there's my horses and gear too, sir," said Riley "you see . . ."

"That will be looked into too, Riley," said the sub-inspector, who now looked as though he was trying to restrain himself from breaking into laughter.

Riley didn't care much any more. All he wanted to do was to lie down somewhere and go to sleep. Surely this must all be straightened out somehow; he couldn't possibly be convicted of horse stealing and sent to gaol. Somewhere in the Colony there must be some saner authority than this sadistic fool sunk into the chair in front of him.

Seven days in the cells and Riley, sallow from want of sunlight and sick from prison food, was brought before the sub-inspector again. Was it really necessary, he thought irritably, for a trooper to stand on either side of him like that? He was hardly likely to assault the sub-inspector, although it was an attractive idea.

"I thought, Riley," began the sub-inspector, speaking with a tolerance and geniality that rang false as hell to Riley, "that you'd be interested in the report of the party who investigated your story."

He paused and looked expectantly at Riley. He still had a fleck of foam at the corner of his mouth, thought Riley. He said nothing.

"Well?" barked the sub-inspector.

"Yes, sir," Riley said resignedly.

"Well," said the sub-inspector, genial again: "To begin with they found your camp, more or less where you said it was."

He paused again and leaned forward on his desk, raising his eyebrows to lend force to what he was about to say.

"It was in ashes, Riley, ashes."

He paused again, to let that sink in.

"And they found your horses, Riley. Both shot through the head."

"Then I presume the bushrangers found the camp,

sir," said Riley, "I suppose they would have spent a fair amount of time looking for me, and——"

"You may suppose what you like, Riley," said the sub-inspector harshly. Then dropping his voice so that it was almost a whisper: "All I'm giving you is the facts."

He leaned back in his chair with a smug simper on his face, as though to say, "there what do you think of that?"

This man was a genuine maniac, Riley realised. Not just an irascible eccentric but a lunatic who simply ought to be locked up. And here he was in charge of a body of troopers and with his, Riley's, fate in his power.

"They found the cave you spoke of Riley," continued the sub-inspector, "and some evidence of an explosion. So at least we can assume that some part of your story is true—there was an explosion, eh?"

"And do you know what else they found Riley? Do you know what else they found?"

"No, sir."

"They found a new grave Riley, a new grave."

A grave, then he had killed somebody?

"They dug it up, Riley, and what do you think they found inside? A body, Riley, the body of a man who had been shot in the head."

That dark mass that had screamed when he fired at it on the path on the bridge a week ago; that was the man he'd killed. Riley was aware of no particular emotion.

"And this man, Riley, is no known bushranger. He's not known to the police at all. So what do you make of that? Eh?"

"Well, I presume, sir, that he's just a member of

Hatton's gang. He must recruit new members occasionally. I suppose it's quite possible there are quite a few bushrangers whose identity is not known to the police."

"You suppose a lot, don't you, Riley? Well suppose you just go out now and see if you could identify this man."

"But I couldn't possibly, sir," said Riley.

"What, couldn't even identify the man you shot?"

"But I told you in my report, sir, it was completely dark: I had no idea what he looked like."

"Is that so, Riley?" said the sub-inspector, leaning forward again and leering. "And after the warning I gave you when you started to be careful who you went about shooting."

This was impossible, thought Riley. This couldn't be happening to him.

"There'll have to be an inquest, Riley, an inquest. And wouldn't it be surprising if you found yourself charged with murder as well as horse stealing."

Riley said nothing. There was nothing he could say.

"Very good, Sergeant," said the sub-inspector, "take him out and show him that body."

There was a sweet sick smell in the hot tin shed, empty except for the slab table with its burden of a blanket shrouded mass that looked as though it couldn't possibly be the body of a man.

This was a man he'd killed, thought Riley, but still there was no reaction. This was all too remote from the frantic action on the ridge. There was no longer any relationship between himself and this man, this body. Not that there ever had been much.

The trooper pulled back the blanket and Riley saw

the remains of a human face, badly torn about and almost black with dried blood.

"What did you hit him with," said the sergeant, speaking for the first time. "A shotgun?"

So it was the bird shot that had done the job. Riley thought, he might have realised he would have missed with the ball.

"No," he said, "I had a pistol loaded with birdshot."

"Must have been pretty close," said the Sergeant.

"Yes," said Riley.

The corpse's head was almost bare of hair, and Riley remembered seeing the bald headed man in the fire-light when he was crouching in the cave. That gave the corpse some identity, gave Riley some feeling of actually having killed someone—not a faceless blur in the dark that had become a faceless corpse in a tin shed. Some feeling, but not much. It was all too academic now, and too complicated with absurdities.

"Do you know 'im?" asked the Sergeant.

"No." said Riley.

"Pity you didn't get the Hangman," said the Sergeant. "You'd be a rich man."

"Oh?" said Riley, surprised, "You believe me do you?"

"Course I do," said the Sergeant, "Everybody does. Don't worry about old Mad Mick. He'll have to send the report down to Sydney and you'll be out of here in a week."

"Mad Mick?" said Riley, "that's the sub-inspector is it?"

"Yeah. Mad Mick Madden they call him. He'll be relieved soon. He's driving us all as mad as he is.

But you've got nothing to worry about. You've done a good job—for a special that is."

The Sergeant pulled the blanket over the corpse's face.

"What about the inquest he's talking about?"

"Oh there'll be an inquest all right, but the verdict'll be justifiable homicide. You've got nothing at all to worry about."

"What about that girl?" said Riley, "The sub-inspector didn't say anything about her. Did they talk to her?"

"Janey Cabel? They talked to her all right, but she had six witnesses to swear she was at a dance in the shanty all that night. But don't worry about that. Everybody knows young Johnny Cabel's one of the Hangman's telegrams."

The Sergeant seemed disposed to chat, but Riley was finding the atmosphere of the shed oppressive, even more so than that of his cell.

"That's not a bad idea," said the Sergeant as he locked the door on Riley. "Putting bird shot in pistols. I'll pass that on."

It was another two weeks before the order for Riley's release came up from Sydney, despite the fact that the Coroner's inquest had, as the Sergeant predicted, brought in a verdict of justifiable homicide.

"You've been more fortunate than you deserve, Riley," said the sub-inspector, and there was no suggestion of geniality about him now.

"Yes, sir," said Riley, who didn't agree at all. Rather the reverse in fact.

"I have been instructed to re-equip you and send you out again," said the sub-inspector, mumbling and speaking more to the desk in front of him than to Riley.

"Yes, sir," said Riley.

"However," said the sub-inspector, looking up at Riley and speaking more clearly and with more relish: "I have had no instructions as to either your pay or your gear and in the absence of any other advice propose to act according to the regulations."

"Oh," said Riley, not knowing what acting according to regulations involved but assuming it must be unpleasant.

"You will therefore have the value of your horses and gear debited against you and the amount taken from your pay. You know how much that is, Riley?"

"No, sir."

"Ninety-four pounds seventeen shillings, Riley. Ninety-four pounds seventeen shillings."

"Yes, sir."

"However the regulations provide that the whole of a trooper's pay shall not be deducted to defray the expenses of replacing equipment lost or damaged," said the sub-inspector, speaking from the book as he was occasionally prone to.

"You will therefore be allowed to retain fifty per cent of your pay each month."

At that rate it would take him roughly a year before he received full pay again, Riley calculated rapidly. It was obviously time he left the service. There must be some other way he could make a living in the colony. He couldn't think of one offhand though. Still, it meant he now had eight pounds, which was something.

"However," continued the sub-inspector, "as you have spent three quarters of your first month in the service in prison, you will draw only one week's wages this month. You will be allowed to retain fifty per cent."

This could all be corrected, thought Riley. A written complaint to headquarters in Sydney would set all this right. But how long would it take, and what fantastic amount of trouble would it involve? Better just get out of the service now and forget the whole thing.

"And in case you were thinking of leaving us, Riley," said the sub-inspector, "I might remind you that in the event of a trooper leaving the service the whole of any money due under the provisions for the replacement of gear lost or damaged becomes due immediately."

This bloody man seemed to be reading his thoughts.

"And I might also remind you Riley that leaving the service without due notice constitutes desertion and is punishable by imprisonment. Imprisonment, Riley."

"Yes, sir." The situation seemed well covered from any possible angle. God damn the impulse that had brought him to this barbaric Colony and double God damn the impulse that had led him to join the police force.

"So off you go again, Riley, and if you can't bring back a bushranger at least bring back a better story next time, eh?"

The sub-inspector's uncontrolled laughter followed Riley out of the office.

Riley hoped he choked.

The small boys followed Riley out of town again.

He was equipped exactly as he had been a month before, even down to the horses, who surely must have been foaled by the same dams as the other two, and as long ago.

The only difference was that this time Riley was reading and re-reading a letter which had been handed to him when he collected his gear. It had been waiting at the barracks for him for a fortnight, but he hadn't been able to receive it while he was in the cells.

"Dear Mr. Riley," the letter ran: "I understand it is you whom I have to thank for the recovery of my racehorse Cicero. I understand your present circumstances make it impractical for me to thank you personally at the moment, but I also understand these circumstances are only of a temporary, formal nature. I would be more than grateful if, as soon as you are able, you would call at my property to enable me to express my thanks in a concrete form."

The letter was signed Charles Collingwood, and underneath the signature was a small map showing how to reach his property from the township of Goulburn.

Now just what did Charles Collingwood mean by a "concrete form" Riley wondered as he walked his horses slowly along the first of the roads indicated by the map. The racehorse was undoubtedly a valuable animal and there well could have been a reward offered for its recovery. How much? Fifty pounds perhaps, a hundred? Anyhow it was obviously well worth going to see him. At least he might get a decent meal, of which he felt sorely in need.

The homestead was about a mile off the road and the drive up to it was lined with pines about ten years old. The homestead itself was a long, wooden building painted white with verandahs on all sides. Hundreds of sheep were grazing in paddocks around the house, although the house itself was isolated in a garden of lawns and shrubs from which the sheep were barred by a white picket fence.

It was a pleasanter place than Riley had seen since he arrived in Australia, except for a few stone houses near the port in Sydney.

He left his horses outside the homestead garden and walked up a metal drive to the house.

"That's quite far enough for the time being," a voice called to him.

He stopped walking. He could see no-one.

"What's your name?" came the voice.

"Dermot Riley."

"And what's your business?"

"I was invited here by a Mr. Collingwood," said Riley.

"My dear fellow," cried the voice apologetically, "I'm so sorry." A door on the verandah opened and a tall, lean man, dressed in white, and carrying a double-barrelled shot-gun, came out.

"Come in my dear fellow," he said, advancing across the verandah, "I'm most terribly sorry. I didn't remember the name. I'm Collingwood." He offered his hand which Riley duly shook.

"Come on inside. Don't worry about your horses, I'll get someone to look after them. Come on in."

He led Riley into a hallway in which the most outstanding piece of furniture was a rack holding every type of firearm Riley had ever heard of and some that he hadn't.

Collingwood carefully placed the shot gun in a vacant slot in the rack.

"This sort of thing is a bit dramatic, but quite necessary out here at the moment as you'll appreciate," he said. Riley was trying to place Collingwood's accent. He spoke perfect English, but it had a clipped and pure quality that made it unlike any English Riley had heard spoken. The man didn't look English. He was very fair and had a small shaped beard that came to a point only an inch or so beyond his chin. It was hard to tell what age he was, but he certainly wasn't over fifty.

"That's quite an armoury you have there," said Riley.

"Yes, I know," said Collingwood apologetically, "but then we have to. We've had bushrangers out here twice, you know. The second time they got Cicero. I'm inclined to think they'll have another try for him too. But for Heaven's sake man, don't let's stand talking here. Come and have a drink inside. Why don't you take your sword off and hang it here. It must be a damned uncomfortable thing to wear all the time if you don't mind my saying so." He spoke very rapidly, but so clearly that Riley had no difficulty following him.

Riley unbuckled his sword and Collingwood took it from him and hung it on the arms rack. He had very long, thin hands, Riley saw, which looked as though they had seldom been used for hard work.

Collingwood led him into a room off the hall with windows so heavily draped that it was quite gloomy. Riley was aware of an unfamiliar sensation about his feet and looked down to see that he was walking on thick carpet. Carpet indeed, this Collingwood must really have money.

Collingwood drew back a curtain and ushered Riley into one of the deep chairs which, with a couple of heavy oak sideboards and a vast table, made up the furniture of the room.

"Now," Collingwood was saying, "I have something here which I think might gladden your heart a little." He was pouring liquid into glasses from a bottle he'd taken from one of the sideboards.

"There now," said Collingwood, handing him a glass, "I'll guarantee you haven't tasted that since you've been in the Colony."

Riley cautiously sipped at the liquid. It was Irish whisky. Delightful.

"You are Irish aren't you?" asked Collingwood, "A Dublin man if I'm not mistaken?"

Riley was surprised. Few foreigners recognised his particular accent as Irish. Most people took him for North American. He said as much to Collingwood.

"Well of course the name helped me a lot," said Collingwood modestly. "But now my dear fellow, tell me the whole story of your encounter with this Hatton man. I know a lot of it, in fact it's fact becoming a legend, but tell me yourself, how did you get on to him in the first place?"

Riley loved talking to an appreciative audience and he loved whisky. The bottle was well diminished by the time he finished telling the story, which, he reflected a little ashamedly, had gained considerably by what the bottle had lost.

"And they actually kept you in gaol for three weeks," Collingwood was saying incredulously. "That man Madden is becoming altogether impossible. There's quite a move on to get rid of him, you know."

"No. I didn't know," said Riley, "but I'm quite in favour of it."

"He's been absolutely useless as far as cleaning out

the bushrangers is concerned, and he's completely demoralised his troopers."

"I'm not surprised," said Riley, "He's demoralised me."

"Oh come," said Collingwood flatteringly, "that I doubt. But tell me my dear fellow — some more whisky?"

"Thanks."

"Tell me what brought you out to these wild parts?"

"Oh I don't know," said Riley, "just an urge to wander."

"But why, if you'll forgive me, why into the police force? I mean you're obviously a man of some education . . ."

"For want of something better to do, I suppose," said Riley, quite truthfully this time. Damn this gentleman to gentleman business, he was thinking. If the man offered him a reward now he'd have to refuse, as one gentleman to another. Heaven send Collingwood would be sufficiently insistent for him to give in gracefully.

"Extraordinary," said Collingwood, "still I suppose it's an interesting sort of life, as a short term proposition."

"Oh it's interesting enough," said Riley noncommittally.

"And you're going to keep on at it for a while, are you?"

"For a while," said Riley, thinking grimly of the ninety-four pounds seventeen shillings he had to find before he could leave the service. Pity he hadn't thought of bringing that out when he was telling his story. It hardly seemed decent to raise the matter now.

"And what exactly are your immediate plans?"

To go as long a way as he could into such bush country as he was reasonably sure was free of bush-rangers and rest there for a month, thought Riley, but he said vaguely: "Oh just patrol around I suppose."

"Going to have another go at Hatton?"

"Oh well," said Riley, ambiguously.

"Because I was wondering," said Collingwood, hesitating, "That is if you wouldn't be offended . . ."

Here it comes, thought Riley, striving to look as much as possible like a man who wouldn't be offended by anything.

"It seems to me that all you trooper people are shockingly badly equipped and I was wondering if, by way of a token of my appreciation of your recovering Cicero for me, you would, as a special favour to me, mind accepting . . ."

Get on with it man, thought Riley, I'll accept a lot as a special favour to you. Ninety-four pounds seventeen shillings preferably.

Collingwood was obviously suffering some embarrassment in making his offer of a reward and Riley knew with despair that he'd have to display equally gentlemanly and sensitive feelings and refuse it.

But the offer when it finally came surprised him.

". . . mind accepting say, a revolver and breech loading rifle from me. I'd be most grateful if you would."

"Well I . . ." began Riley, calculating with one part of his mind what the sale value of such articles would be and with another knowing shame at his churlish reception of what was in fact a generous and delicate offer.

"After all," Collingwood continued. "It's nothing short of disgraceful that you should be expected to fight with the antiquated things you're issued with. And after all, it's people like myself that you're protecting, and it's really no more than common sense on my part to supply you with the proper tools, quite apart from my personal obligation to you."

"Well," said Riley, "it's very good of you, but . . ."

"Please," said Collingwood, "I insist."

"Well then," said Riley. "If you insist."

"Excellent!" said Collingwood, and then as if inspired by his success: "and look, you don't have any particular plan of campaign do you?"

"No, not exactly," said Riley puzzled.

"I mean you just go out on patrol and more or less see what you can run into, don't you?"

Or away from, thought Riley, "More or less."

"Well, why don't you make this place your base for a few months. I mean you're right in the heart of the bushranger country. You could cover the whole district in one or two day rides from here."

"Well I . . ." began Riley.

"And you could use my horses, which means you'd be able to cover a lot more territory." Riley realised with surprise that the man was desperately in earnest, he really wanted him to stay.

"But surely I'd be in the way, after all, a stranger . . ."

"Not at all," said Collingwood hastily. "Quite the contrary. As a matter of fact my wife and daughters are in Europe and won't be back for at least six months. You'd be more than welcome."

"Well, that's very kind of you." Camping had never been to Riley's taste, and the idea of sleeping in a bed regularly appealed strongly.

"You will then?"

"Well I . . ."

"You will?"

"Well thank you very much. Yes, I will." What else could he say?

Riley slept deeply and well that night in a feather bed.

He spent the next couple of days practising with his new weapons. After firing about fifty rounds from the revolver he found that if he fired at a tree roughly the width of a man and no more than fifty feet away he stood a reasonable chance of hitting at least some part of it, and was almost certain to hit it if he fired all five shots in the magazine. With the rifle he became reasonably expert, and once even hit a running rabbit at something like one hundred and fifty feet. None of which was exactly brilliant, he thought, but at least his chances of survival were increased if he were involved in another battle. Secretly he preferred the idea of a pistol loaded with bird shot because that, at close range, stood an excellent chance of taking effect provided it were pointed in the general direction of its target. But the mechanism of the revolver would take only made up ammunition—bullet, charge and cap—and he didn't like to experiment with powder and shot for fearing of damaging the barrel of that very valuable weapon.

Riley spent a lot of his time riding around the property with Collingwood. He was particularly impressed with the fact that Collingwood's work consisted entirely of giving general instructions to his workmen who, in their turn, seemed to do relatively little in the way of work. Sheep, it appeared, made their owners quite rich without any great effort on the part of the owner.

It was different at shearing time, Collingwood assured him, but, when pressed, he admitted that shearing time did not come round all that often. If by any particularly unkind stroke of fate he were forced to remain in the Colony indefinitely, Riley decided, he would take up sheep farming.

In the evenings Collingwood and Riley drank whisky, which was apparently available in unlimited quantities, and Collingwood did his best to find out something of Riley's past life, in which he was quite unsuccessful. Riley, on the other hand, learned that Collingwood was a Swede, his real name was Oestman, but he had taken on his wife's name because he was tired of explaining how to spell his own. He had spent a great deal of his life in England and had come out to Australia ten years ago to take up sheep farming on the strength of the success John Macarthur had had in developing a variation on Spanish sheep.

"It's all been very successful but the girls" — in the "girls" he included his wife along with the two daughters—"were getting restless so I thought I'd let them go back for a while to see that they weren't really missing anything. It doesn't take all that long now that the steamers are running." The girls had been gone eighteen months.

"You don't miss Europe yourself?" Riley asked.

"What is there to miss? Cold? Snow? Fog? Cities that belch smoke all day and all night. Traffic so thick it's dangerous to cross a road. Look at that . . ." he gestured out a window to the clear starlit night—

"How could a man live with that and miss anything in Europe?"

Riley, who, if he allowed himself, could feel desperately homesick for snow and cold and wet grey skies and the pinched blue faces of his fellow Dubliners, did not agree, but he didn't argue.

"What about the bushrangers?" he asked. "Don't you find them something of a strain?"

"I look on them as a sort of occupational risk," said Collingwood seriously: "If you're properly armed and look out for yourself they're not all that much of a worry. If I were living in one of the tropical colonies I'd have to take precautions against disease. Here it's just a different type of pestilence. And I put it to you that in India the plague and the cholera kill off a lot more colonists than the bushrangers do here."

"Mm," said Riley, unconvinced.

"Besides," said Collingwood, expansively, pouring more whisky. "Bushranging is just a phase. A few more years'll see the end of it. Gardiner's in gaol. Morgan's dead. They killed Ben Hall only a few months ago over at Forbes."

"There seems to be plenty more to take their place," said Riley.

"But few of the stature, if you can use that word, of men like Gardiner and Hall. Most of them are just bush louts that don't last more than a month or two anyway. It's when you get men gaining reputations and gathering followers around them that you get real trouble."

"Like Hatton," said Riley.

"Like Hatton. Once Hatton goes, you watch. Bushranging will die out here like—like——" he waved his glass in the air seeking a simile—"like blowflies in the winter."

A dog barked briefly and both men sat quietly in their chairs, the thought of Hatton still uppermost in their minds.

"It's nothing," said Collingwood after a moment. "There's six dogs out there and if there were any strangers around we'd know it. Here, let me fill your glass."

"By the way, did it ever occur to you that it would be a good idea for you to shave your beard off?"

"No. Why?" said Riley fingering his chin defensively.

"Well everybody in Goulburn knows what happened up there on Lightning Fork Ridge."

"So?"

"So if everybody in Goulburn knows you can guarantee that Hatton knows."

"Oh. So?"

"So Hatton is famous for being a very vengeful man."

"But then I doubt that many people in Goulburn would have any idea what I look like?"

"No. But what about Janey Cabel?"

"Yes. I wonder. She wouldn't have a very clear idea, though," said Riley.

"Would she recognise you if she met you again do you think?"

Riley realised that he still carried a very clear memory of the girl's face, lit by the fire, her mouth open to scream; but then he had seen her before. Come to think of it, she had seen him before too.

"I don't know. She might at that."

"Here, have another drink. No, what I was thinking was that it might be amusing for you to shave your beard off, cut your hair differently, possibly even dye it, change your clothes entirely—I can fix that for you—and go out to the shanty and have a talk to Janey."

"What on earth for?" said Riley, appalled.

"Well, you might get a lead on Hatton," said Collingwood.

Riley was about to repudiate the very notion that he was not simply a semi-permanent guest in Collingwood's home. The idea had been that he should use it as a base for his bushranger patrols.

"Hm, yes," he said thoughtfully.

"As a matter of fact," said Collingwood, warming to his subject. "It has occurred to me that we might be able to lay Mr. Hatton by the heels ourselves."

"Oh?"

"You consider. Suppose you, as a stranger, drop into the shanty and let it be known that you're working on my property. Go a couple of times, pretend to get drunk, get a name for yourself as a talkative fellow; then just drop it around where Janey can hear you that I keep a lot of rough gold on the premises, or better still that I've been dealing in gold and usually have a lot of it on the premises on Friday nights. I'll wager we have Hatton and his crew out here the following Friday.'

What a weird ambition, thought Riley, but all he said was: "Can I have another drink?"

"Of course, here help yourself. But you see what I mean? You and I could lie in wait for them, lock up the dogs so that they can come right in and then, well, we'll work out the details later, but you see what I mean."

"Yes," said Riley sadly, "I see what you mean."

"Of course we could get some troopers in to help us," said Collingwood, "but I don't feel that we're likely to get any sensible co-operation from that man Madden, do you?"

"No," said Riley.

"Right. Then you feel we should go it alone, eh?"

Riley didn't see that that was necessarily the only alternative, but felt that now he'd been hopelessly forced into a false position.

"And do you really think it would be essential that I shave?"

"I think it would be wise. Anyhow it's getting quite fashionable now. You'll see quite a few clean shaven men around Sydney."

Riley looked into the sparkling blue eyes of the expatriate Swede and couldn't bring himself to argue against all that wholesome bloodthirsty enthusiasm.

"They usually have a sort of dance at the shanty on Saturday nights," Collingwood was saying. "You could start working your way in then."

Riley started to say that he didn't care for dancing, but then realised that that was irrelevant. Perhaps he had drunk too much whisky. He poured himself another glass.

They went to bed very late that night and Riley awoke next morning with the curiously purified feeling that comes from having drunk too much Irish whisky. He also woke with a hazy recollection of Collingwood, towards the end of the evening, having advanced the suggestion that, when the bushrangers responded to the bait, they be met with an expanded version of Riley's cave mining device. That at least, Riley felt, could be disregarded on the grounds that it would almost certainly result in the homestead being blown to matchwood.

But the rest of it — what had he agreed to last night? Riley buried his face in the pillow and groaned softly.

Diffidently Riley drew the razor down his heavily lathered cheek. It sliced through the hair remarkably easily. Stroke by stroke there was revealed to Riley a face that was still surprisingly like the face he remembered in the days of his youth, before it had finally become submerged in a decent veil of hair. The chin was rather too long for the other features, and his mouth now seemed abnormally wide. Moreover his nose seemed to stick out more. The whole thing had been better balanced with the beard, he thought sorrowfully. For a moment he toyed with the idea of retaining a moustache, but decided that it made his mouth look even wider than it was.

When he wiped away the remnants of lather he found the newly shaven parts of his face were a different colour from the rest. A sort of pale ghost of his beard remained. Perhaps that would be an excuse for putting off his visit to the shanty for another week.

But by the end of the week the sun and wind had done their work and Riley's face was the even copper colour of the other inhabitants of the southern tablelands.

CHAPTER FOUR

ANYHOW, HE TOLD HIMSELF as he jogged down the road towards Lightning Fork on a superb gelding that Collingwood had lent him, anyhow nothing much would happen that night. All he had to do was drink too much and let it be known that he worked at Collingwood's. He had no fear of the girl's recognising him. In fact he was so confident of his changed appearance that he was seriously thinking of deserting the police service secure in the knowledge that nobody would be able to recognise him to charge him with desertion or to claim the money he so unjustly owed. But then that might cause undue complication when he wanted to leave the Colony.

Riley heard the sounds of dancing long before the shanty itself came into sight. There were a couple of fiddles, being played incredibly quickly, laughter and loud voices, snatches of song, and across the lot like a blanket of sound the regular crash of boots on a wooden floor. Two light crashes and one heavy, as though the dancers were taking two preparatory hops before leaping high in the air and dashing their feet to the boards in unison. Which was more or less what they were doing, Riley found, when he arrived at the shanty.

Several fires had been lit on the cleared ground in front of the shanty and lanterns had been hung on lines running from nearby trees to the building itself. The barrels and boxes Riley had seen before inside the shanty were now outside, half of them occupied by men who stamped their feet on the ground and banged their pint pots on the barrels in time with the music. The door of the shanty was wide open and the smoky glare inside showed the place crammed with wildly dancing couples. Riley guessed that the men sitting outside had been unable to secure partners. There was sure to be a shortage of women at this sort of thing.

The noise level was almost unbelievable and it

seemed to Riley that the whole shanty shook and trembled to the rhythm of the music and the crashing feet. It possibly did. A couple of men in white aprons emerged from the shanty with trays of beer and began serving the drinkers sitting outside. One of them told Riley to tether his horse round the back of the shanty, but he decided to take it across to the scrub on the other side of the road. He didn't anticipate trouble, but if there were any he didn't want to scramble for his horse amongst the confusion of buggies, traps and hacks that he supposed he would find behind the shanty.

As he walked back towards the building it struck Riley that the scene outside, the men sitting at barrels, the flickering yellow light everywhere, the gay strains of music and the shouts and laughter, created an atmosphere not unlike that of the outdoor drinking places he'd seen in France and Spain. This one certainly had a personality of its own, but the principle was the same. It would be interesting to see whether this Colony eventually developed an English or Continental tradition in its social habits.

Personally Riley disliked the whole thing. His tradition was in the nature of friends gathering at each other's homes to sing and drink and to talk. He saw no point in gathering together a crowd of strangers, or comparative strangers, with liquor and noise their greatest bonds.

Probably this place would go the way of the Continent, he thought morosely. The climate would make for this sort of outdoor life, and there were certainly enough Europeans here already.

Riley sat down on one of the boxes and bought a pot of beer from a waiter. He determined to make it last all evening because he was not going to make vast inroads on the only two pounds he had in the world. He had only to pretend to be drinking too much anyway. It was unlikely that anybody would notice how much he actually drank and besides, there was no way of telling that he hadn't been drinking heavily long before he came here.

Soon the dancing inside reached a crescendo, then stopped abruptly, and couples began to spill out of the shanty.

Two young men, hand in hand with a couple of girls, claimed the barrel at which Riley was sitting. He abandoned it gracefully, and drifted into the shanty. He wanted to see whether Janey Cabel was there anyway.

The floor of the shanty had been cleared apart from a platform made of beer barrels and planks at one end. That would be for the fiddlers, Riley thought. The fiddlers themselves, instruments in their hands, were at the bar, and, Good God, there was the old man, still in the same place, still motionless. Not *still* Riley corrected himself, *again* surely. He couldn't have been there since Riley saw him last. But the effect was eerie, particularly when he heard the old man's voice replying to some remark by one of the musicians. As before there was no visible movement among the hair that hung round his mouth.

Riley walked over to the bar and set his pot down. The musicians glanced at him and one nodded, but the old man never stirred.

Riley wondered how he was supposed to go about introducing himself into this circle. No-one seemed remotely interested in him. Probably the best would be to ask somebody to dance, but then there seemed to be such a dire shortage of women that he'd probably get killed in the rush.

The two fiddlers downed their beer and tramped back to their improvised stands. Riley wondered what they did when they weren't fiddling. Probably station hands. Most of the men here looked as though they could be station hands.

The fiddlers looked at each other, nodded and then broke into a frenzy of sawing at their instruments. The sharp vivid sounds seemed to physically draw the dancers into the shanty and in moments the whole place was again full of couples, jigging and twirling. Riley eased himself into a corner made by the bar and one wall of the shanty.

He saw Jane Cabel dancing with a tall, clean shaven young man. She looked rather ill, he thought. He wondered whether the young man was one of her bushranger friends. Quite possibly there were a number of bushrangers in this gathering, amateurs or professionals. The shanty had become hot and stuffy with the influx of the crowd and Riley began to wish he'd stayed outside.

There seemed to be some sort of disturbance near the doorway. The people there had stopped dancing. Probably someone had fallen over. Or perhaps it was a fight. Riley couldn't see very clearly.

Then the dancers in the middle of the shanty stopped and some of the men cursed someone who was trying to struggle through the crowd. One of the fiddlers stopped playing, then started again, but out of time now with his companion.

There was a fight. A thin young fellow was struggling with another older man. The young one broke away, and pushed through the crowd. One of the dancers shoved violently at him and he reeled, then scrambled on. The man he'd been fighting was thrusting through the crowd after him.

The young man reached the bar and scrambled over it, near the old shanty-owner, who still didn't move.

Then astonishingly, the young man grabbed the shanty-owner's arm and hung on to it. His face was distorted and wet with tears.

Riley recognised him then. It was the youth who'd tried to hold him up when he was riding out along the road from Goulburn.

The shanty was in an uproar now. A few determined couples were still trying to dance in the far corner, but most were staring at the tableau in front of the bar. The old man, motionless, leaning on his elbows; the youth cringing behind the bar, clinging to his father and weeping . . . the man who'd been chasing him standing with the palms of his hands on the bar as though to vault over.

One of the fiddlers cut out again; the other struggled on alone for a few moments then his scraping too died away.

There was some sort of confusion in the doorway again, Riley could hardly see over the heads of the crowd, but more men seemed to be coming in and forcing their way through.

The harsh voice of the old shanty-owner sounded over the babble of talk and scraping feet: "Just stay where you are Martin Kingston. Just stay where you are."

He seemed to be talking to the man who was threatening to leap over the bar. The man answered, but Riley, who was only ten feet away, couldn't hear him.

The crowd began to fall back from the middle of the shanty and Riley saw half a dozen men, revolvers in hand, coming through towards the bar.

Leading them was James Hatton, huge and bearded, a revolver in each hand and several more stuck in his belt.

Riley for a moment regretted the revolver he'd left in his saddle bag, then was glad he had because otherwise he might have been tempted to do something absurd. Not that the temptation would have been great. The crowd was falling back before the armed men and Riley found himself crushed into the corner, finding it difficult to breathe, much less move. But because of his position against the bar he could now see quite clearly everything that was happening.

The men with Hatton spread out on either side of him, urging the crowd back towards the walls. A few women screamed, but everybody moved back, the men warily eyeing the revolvers being aimed at their stomachs.

The man who'd been chasing Johnny Cabel, Riley remembered that that was the youth's name, fell back when Hatton approached.

Hatton stopped within a few feet of the bar. He gestured at the cringing boy, but spoke to his father.

"I want him, Dan," Hatton said, his deep vibrant voice rising clear above the noises in the shanty. As he spoke everyone fell silent and still, as though striving to listen.

"Why?" came the harsh gravelly monosyllable from the old man. Riley realised that the old man's head, bent over the bar as he was, was still on a level with Hatton's. And Hatton, he knew, was six foot three.

"He's a traitor," said Hatton. The youth had stopped

whimpering now and was staring fixedly at Hatton. He still clung to his father's arm, like a small boy.

"Why do you say that?" said the old man, who still had not changed his position.

The bushranger seemed to be treating old Cabel with some respect, thought Riley. Jane Cabel squirmed out of the crowd at the far end of the shanty and made her way to the bar. None of the bushrangers interfered with her. She stood in front of the bar in front of Hatton.

"Yes, why do you say that, James Hatton?" she said bravely enough, thought Riley. But she looked white and drawn. Perhaps she was sick.

"I'm sorry about this, Janey," said Hatton, "but he had something to do with that business up at the cave."

Riley saw for the first time that there was a livid, fresh scar, running from the bushranger's temple to his chin, cleaving a line through his beard. Had Riley done that with his sword? Had Hatton been the anonymous rider he'd struck down on Lightning Fork Ridge?

"He did not," cried Jane Cabel: "Did you, Johnny?" She turned to her brother.

John Cabel shook his head.

"There, you see," said Jane to Hatton, as though something had been proved.

Hatton motioned with his hand to one of his followers and the man went over and stood by the door leading out into the kitchen.

"Come out here, Johnny," said Hatton, "I want to talk to you."

"You can talk to him from there," said the old man. Hatton hesitated. Riley wondered what it was that made him respect the shanty owner. It couldn't be his sheer size. The man was enormous, but he was very old. And Hatton was armed.

"You set the traps on us, didn't you, Johnny?" said Hatton at last.

"No, Jim. I didn't. I swear I didn't."

"Then where've you been the last month?"

"Just knockin' around, doin' a bit of work on me own."

Hatton stared at the boy. He said nothing for a moment and then he turned to the crowd.

"We're going to have a trial here," he announced: "We're going to try Johnny Cabel for treachery. If he's found guilty we're going to hang him." There was a stir in the crowd and Riley became aware that the man standing next to him, a stout man, was very red in the face and was breathing heavily. Riley hoped he wasn't going to be sick.

"These men," continued Hatton, gesturing with a revolver at his followers, "are going to be the jury. I'm going to be the judge. You—" he waved his revolver generally at the crowd—"you're the audience and can see fair play."

The man had no sense of humour, thought Riley.

Hatton leaned back against the bar and let the barrels of his revolvers point to the ground.

"Now you all know, or you ought to know that Johnny Cabel here was one of us." Riley took that to mean that Cabel had been a member of the gang. Why was the bushranger going through this pantomime, he wondered. It looked as though he was simply trying to justify himself in front of the old man, or the crowd, or both.

"And you all know what happened up on Lightning Fork Ridge. We were ambushed by a bunch of Traps."

That was flattering, thought Riley.

"We drove the dingoes off, as we always will," said Hatton, "but they killed Mick Ramsden."

So that was the man's name. First the memory of having seen him by the fire, and now learning his name, Riley felt as though the man he had killed was being created in his memory. He shook his head to clear the thought away.

"Now we have reason to believe that Johnny Cabel, here, told those Traps where we were."

"But he didn't," cried Jane — "he didn't, he didn't."

Hatton ignored her.

"Now we admit we could be wrong about that."

You don't, you liar, thought Riley.

"And that's why we're holding this trial. We want to make sure." A half-remembered quotation came to Riley's mind. "I beseech you in the bowels of Christ to admit you might be wrong." Who said that? Oliver Cromwell wasn't it? Not exactly a tolerant man either. Riley wondered whether Cromwell had been prompted by a sentiment similar to Hatton's. He probably was. And the expression of his tolerance was likely to be much the same. Would they really hang the boy? And what was the old man thinking about all this? He was still leaning there motionless. There was something purely affected about that immobility.

"Now, Johnny," said Hatton, turning to the boy who was now standing upright, not clinging to his father, but very close to him. "You say you didn't set the Traps on us?"

"No, I didn't," said John, with just a touch of defiance.

"You didn't tell anybody where Lightning Fork *plant* was?"

"No I didn't, Jim. Honest, Jim I didn't. I don't know why you think I did."

Hatton turned again to the crowd.

"Now you all heard that. Johnny here says he never set the Traps on, us, right?"

He turned again to John Cabel.

"Now when did you first hear about this business up on the Ridge?"

"Aw, I dunno, Jim. A week or two after it happened. Heard some fellers talking about it out at Rushton's shanty. Something in the papers about it they said."

"That's right," said Hatton, talking to the crowd at large again: "There was something in the papers about it. Lies they were. There was a whole bunch of troopers up there."

Riley hadn't known he'd made the newspapers. He must look them up when he went back to Goulburn.

"Now," said Hatton, "you all heard Johnny here say that the first he heard about that business was a week after it happened. Right?"

He turned back to John Cabel.

"Where's your pistol, Johnny?"

Riley saw at last what the bushranger was getting at. He watched Cabel's face but saw only blankness there. Of course the boy would have no way of anticipating what was in the bushranger's mind.

"I left it out in the bush," said the boy. "Don't want to be seen carting a gun around. I been into Goulburn."

Oh futile, futile lie, thought Riley. The boy would have done far better to have told part of the truth and say it had been taken from him by a man he'd tried to hold up. But the boy didn't know what was coming.

"You all hear that?" Hatton asked the crowd: "He says he left his pistol out in the bush." He turned again to Cabel: "When did you leave it out in the bush?"

"Ah I dunno, Jim, about a week ago I think."

"A week ago, he says," declared Hatton, "You're sure of that now are you, Johnny?"

"Aw, I think so. About a week ago, Jimmy."

"Well it wasn't more than a fortnight ago, eh?"

"No, it wouldn't be more than a fortnight." Surely the boy could see he was being led into something, thought Riley.

"All right then," said Hatton, "Now you all heard that, now listen to this."

Ceremoniously he pushed one of his revolvers into his belt and drew out a pistol.

"That's yours isn't it?" he said, holding it out to the boy.

"Aw, I dunno, Jim."

"Well take it and have a look at it. Look at this." With his revolver Hatton pointed to something on the butt of the pistol. Possibly even the boy's name or initials, thought Riley.

The boy didn't take the proffered weapon. He moved a little closer to his father.

"Yes, it's mine," he said sullenly.

"So it's yours, eh?" said Hatton: "And do you know how I got it? I found it on the ridge the night the Traps set on us. This was what killed Mick Ramsden, Your pistol, Johnny. Your pistol."

There was a murmur in the crowd and Riley realised that Hatton had in fact succeeded in creating something of the atmosphere of a courtroom. More-over there was something entirely theatrical about Hatton, although he obviously took himself deadly seriously.

"Well, what have you got to say about that, John-ny?"

"I don't know how it got there," said the boy, slightly tearful now.

"But you were lying when you said you hid it in the bush weren't you?" said Hatton triumphantly.

The boy could still lie his way out of this, thought Riley, if he had his wits about him; but then he didn't seem particularly intelligent. Quite the reverse in fact. And there was something in his face that seemed to be determining his doom, something besides the ab-ject fear. It was shame, Riley realised, the boy was genuinely ashamed of what he had done, and that shame would surely ruin him.

"You were lying, weren't you?" roared Hatton. Everybody was silent now, staring at the guilt stricken face of John Cabel. Even his sister was staring at him doubtfully.

"Not exactly, Jim," said the boy at last, muttering so that Riley could hardly hear him. "Not exactly; you see a cove took it off me."

"I'll say a cove took it off you — it was the cove who owned this, wasn't it?"

Hatton produced yet another pistol from his belt. Riley couldn't see it very clearly, but he guessed what it was.

"It was the cove who owned this, wasn't it?" re-peated Hatton, "and you know what this is don't you: it's a Trap's pistol!" Hatton in some ways was not unlike his sub-inspector thought Riley, except that Hatton was possibly more reasonable.

"All right, Jim," said the boy miserably, "I'll tell you how it was. I held this cove up, or tried to, and he beat me up and took me gun. That's the way it was, Jim, honest it was."

"Then why did you lie about it?" said Hatton.

There was an easy answer to that, thought Riley. He just had to say he'd been ashamed to admit his pistol had been taken from him. These men just might understand and believe that. They'd laugh at him, but they mightn't hang him. But the boy just stood silent, deep shame and guilt evident in the very slouch of his shoulders.

Riley looked at Jane Cabel. She seemed utterly bewildered.

"Johnny," she said, "didn't . . ."

"Oh yes he did," said Hatton: "I can tell you what happened. The Traps caught him and he bought his way out by splitting on us. That's happened. Did they promise you blood money as well if they shot me, Johnny?"

The boy just stood where he was, his face white, his eyes staring. The old man beside him was looking steadily at Hatton.

"Now then," said Hatton, turning to his men: "That's the evidence, what's the verdict?"

His men, who didn't seem to have the same uninhibited sense of drama as Hatton, shuffled their feet and looked self-conscious.

"What's the verdict, I said?" repeated Hatton, loudly.

"Er, guilty, Jim," said one of the bushrangers, looking at his feet.

"Guilty it is!" roared Hatton: "And now the sentence . . ." He turned to John Cabel and pointed one of the revolvers at him. He's going to shoot him, thought Riley, he's going to shoot him dead in cold blood. If he'd had a revolver then he would have started shooting himself, he thought, five shots against seven men. The odds were he would have hit five of them at that range. And surely the crowd would join him then. But it wouldn't have been possible anyway, he was so tightly jammed into the corner he could not even raise his hands from his sides.

"The sentence," Hatton continued: "Is that you be hanged by the neck until you're dead, and may God have mercy on your soul, because I'll have none on your body."

Jane Cabel screamed and rushed at the bushranger.

"Don't, don't, don't," she cried, beating at his chest, "Let him go, Jim, please let him go."

Hatton pushed her away and one of his men took her outside.

"Get me a rope," said Hatton, and another bushranger went out of the shanty. This couldn't really be going to happen, thought Riley, not before his very eyes.

He looked at the boy. He was standing quite still, but his hand was on his father's arm again. Tears were running down his face. The old man was still staring at Hatton. Suddenly Hatton reached across the bar, grabbed a handful of John Cabel's clothing, and hauled him over.

The boy yelped and tried to cling to his father; but the old man, and it was the first time that Riley had seen him move, twitched his arm and broke the boy's clutch.

At that final act of rejection the boy began to howl

like an animal, softly and mournfully. It was horrible. The boy would have fallen to the ground if Hatton hadn't been holding him.

Irresistibly Riley was reminded of his own treatment of the boy and he felt sick with shame, but then at least he hadn't meant it. This man, incredibly, did.

The man came back with the rope and without any orders from Hatton stood on a chair and dropped one end over a rafter. There was already a noose in the rope. Holding him with only one hand Hatton dragged John Cabel over under the rafter, dropped the noose over his neck and hauled on the rope.

The boy stood upright and clutched at the rope with his hands. Hatton knocked the boy's arms away with his fist.

When the boy could just take his weight on the tips of his toes, Hatton stopped hauling.

Just as I did—thought Riley—perhaps after all . . .

"I want John Cabel to hear this," said Hatton, "and I want you all to hear it too. I play square with any man who plays square with me—but there's only one thing I've got for traps and traitors—and that's this . . ."

Hatton walked abruptly back towards the bar, hauling his rope after him. Riley caught one glimpse of John Cabel's face. Blood was running down his chin, his eyes were wide open and filled with bitter horror. Then Riley shut his eyes. Some women had been screaming, but they stopped. There was a sound like a moan from the crowd too, but then it stopped. Then there was almost silence. And then some horrible, unthinkable sounds. And after a while complete silence. It lasted a long time. And then a long gasp from fifty throats.

Riley opened his eyes.

John Cabel's body was revolving slowly in the air, his neck crooked, his feet a foot from the ground.

Hatton let the rope go and the body fell, the boots and the head making separate thumps on the board floor.

Hatton stalked out of the shanty. His men followed him.

Jane Cabel came running in the door, stopped when she saw her brother, made a strange, frightened sound, then ran through into the kitchen.

The crowd began sidling through the door after the bushrangers. Riley heard the hoofbeats of several horses galloping down the road.

The shanty emptied surprisingly quickly, but Riley stayed where he was.

Old man Cabel stared at the body of his son.

The two men who'd been acting as waiters lingered in the doorway for a moment, but then they too disappeared.

There was a bustle of sound at the back of the shanty, then hoofbeats, and the sound of buggy wheels.

Riley could hear a woman sobbing quite close. Probably Jane Cabel in the kitchen.

It struck Riley that John Cabel might not be dead; that he might have suffocated and could yet be revived. He walked across, his footsteps sounding unnaturally loud and looked at the boy's face. He was indisputably dead.

Jane came out of the backroom and stood in the doorway, gazing fearfully at the body.

"Take me round to him," said the old man. Riley learned then why he had never moved. The girl went behind the bar and the old man put an arm round her shoulders and levered himself along the bar with his other hand.

He appeared to be paralysed from the waist down. He took his hand off the bar and lurched the last couple of steps, then slid down onto the floor beside his son's body, his legs outstretched stiffly.

"Can I help?" said Riley. The girl looked at him for the first time. Her eyes were wide and staring, but, in a way, dull. Poor little waif, thought Riley, poor little bush waif.

"Go away," growled the old man.

Riley went out of the shanty, walked across to his horse, mounted, and rode slowly and thoughtfully back to the Collingwood homestead.

CHAPTER FIVE

"BUT WHAT I CAN'T understand," Riley said to Collingwood next day, "is why Hatton went through all that nonsense. Why didn't he just grab the boy and hang him?"

"I think it was probably exactly as you suggested," said Collingwood, "he wanted to justify himself to the crowd."

"But why should he worry about the crowd? Nobody dared move."

"I think you underrate the need of a man like that has to be thought well of. He wanted to kill young Cabel, but he wanted everybody to think he was justified in doing it. You'll find something of the sort was involved in the way he treated the old man. He knew his reputation would suffer if he used violence on a cripple."

"But surely to God," said Riley, "he must have

realised what the effect of hanging the boy would have on the crowd no matter how he dressed it up. I guarantee there isn't a man who was in that shanty last night who wouldn't shoot Hatton on sight if he had the chance."

"Now there I think you're quite wrong," said Collingwood standing up. "Let's go out on the verandah and let the woman ——" gesturing at the remains of the meal on the table — "clear all this away. There I think you're quite wrong. If you talked to those men or the women for that matter, you'd find there wasn't one who thought that Hatton was in the wrong. They'd say he'd been a bit harsh perhaps, but they'd be on his side."

"Surely not," said Riley, squinting against the glare of the sun from the hot paddocks.

"I think so. You haven't been in the Colony long enough to know just what depth of feeling there is against the informer. They're a queer lot these Australians, very queer."

"Queer perhaps, but no-one's as queer as that," said Riley.

"But you've got to understand just what the local product is. It's only a few years since this was substantially a penal Colony, remember. I don't know what the figures are, but I'd think that most of the native born Australians now had at least one convict parent."

"I don't know that that argues so very much," said Riley.

"I do," said Collingwood. "You take a population made up of what are virtually the rejects of a nation and I think it's only reasonable that they're likely to develop a rather peculiar attitude to life. All this'll change of course, now they've stopped transportation, but the whole effect will linger for a while."

"But damn it all," said Riley, "Sheer common sense would make these people realise that the bushrangers are a lot of murderous louts."

"I've never seen much evidence of common sense in the Colony," said Collingwood. "And besides, it's not all the Australians' fault either. They're stuck out here in the wilds. Most of them are dirt poor. They've no education at all. They've got this general criminal background—serious or otherwise it's still criminal—and the most colourful figures in their lives are the bushrangers and the police. Now you just think for a moment — if you were in their position which would you find preferable? A man like Hatton, or a man like your sub-inspector?"

"That's a nice point," said Riley, "but you're getting away from the main argument, which was whether or not anybody is going to look on Hatton as anything but a wild animal after hanging that boy."

"He's hanged people before, you know," said Collingwood mildly.

"Yes. I was thinking mainly of the people who saw him actually doing it last night."

"Hmm, I doubt it," said Collingwood, "I doubt it very much. In fact do you know who is likely to come out of that whole business worst of all?"

"Well, I would have thought Hatton, but obviously you don't think so."

"No, I think you will."

"Me?"

"When they get round to thinking about it, if they do, that mob will blame you, because you were the man who got the information from the boy."

"Oh come!"

"I'm serious, I tell you. They're a very strange lot these Australians."

"Anyway it hardly matters, since they don't know who I am."

"No, but I'd stay clean shaven if I were you."

He'd have to now anyway, reflected Riley. It would take altogether too long to grow a beard, and he was committed to the intolerable labour of shaving virtually every day of his life from now on.

"I take it," said Collingwood, "that you didn't get far with laying the bait for Hatton."

"I didn't get anywhere at all," said Riley. "I don't know. I doubt that Jane Cabel is likely to be on intimate terms with the Hatton gang after this."

"I wouldn't be sure," said Collingwood.

"Oh nonsense," said Riley: "They hanged her brother, man!"

"Yes, I suppose . . ." Collingwood abandoned the train of his thought: "Although you can rely on the fact that there'd always be somebody at that shanty who would pass information back to Hatton."

"You think I should pursue your plan further then," said Riley, smiling.

"My dear fellow, that's entirely your business. I hope I haven't been giving the impression that I'm trying to interfere . . ." Collingwood seemed genuinely upset.

Riley, who thought quite decidedly that Collingwood had been trying to interfere, but didn't particularly object, said: "Not at all. I was just interested in your opinion, whether you thought this set up would have changed things or not."

"No. I don't think so at all. I don't think it makes

any substantial difference—the girl mightn't be your lead any more, but information dropped at the shanty will still find its way to Hatton. I still think the plan's a good one. Don't you?"

Riley thought the whole thing was too simple and ill conceived, but at least it was a plan, and presumably he ought to be doing something about Hatton. Now there was an interesting development, he was beginning to think he *ought* to do something about Hatton. On reflection he decided he would *like* to do something about Hatton. The man was altogether too full of blood and poison. He ought to be pricked. But Collingwood's scheme seemed improbable. Still, Collingwood was a nice fellow.

"Yes I think it's a good one," said Riley, "I'll drop out there again when things have had time to settle down a bit." Which gave him a perfectly valid excuse to hang around the homestead for another couple of weeks, practising his shooting, chatting to Collingwood, who was proving an increasingly engaging companion, and drinking Irish whisky.

It was in fact three weeks before Riley rode back to the Lightning Fork shanty. This time he rode with the comforting knowledge that he was richer than he had been at any time since he arrived in Sydney. The week before he'd strapped on his sword and his Government issue pistol, and ridden into Goulburn on his police hack—which even showed some signs of briskness after a month on the Collingwood pastures —to make his monthly report.

He'd presented himself at the sub-inspector's office, learned with considerable relief that the sub-inspector was in Sydney, and handed in a written report of his supposed activities for the month. He took a little time to identify his shaven self, but finally the sergeant accepted the fact that he was Dermot Riley.

"What's all this?" asked the Sergeant—the same one who had once acted as prisoner's escort for Riley—fingering the half dozen sheets of paper carefully covered with precise handwriting. The report consisted of an account of Riley's treks into the bush country, his hunt for plants, his method of quartering the countryside to increase the efficiency of his operation, and his cautious questioning of the natives for possible information. The report glided skilfully round the fact that there had been no definite results from his efforts as yet, but ended with the suggestion that something, probably something quite big, could probably be expected reasonably soon.

Riley outlined this briefly for the sergeant.

The sergeant pondered a while and glanced through the report.

"What you mean is you made no contact, eh?" he said at last.

"Well, er . . . yes. More or less."

"Then that's all right," said the Sergeant amiably, initialling the report and stuffing it in a drawer. "Don't know why you didn't just say that. No-one reads these bloody things anyway."

"How long will the sub-inspector be away, Sergeant?" said Riley.

"Don't know," said the sergeant morosely. "Hope he stays away for good. He might too. They called him down to Sydney to give him hell over Jimmy Hatton. You heard about Jimmy's latest, I suppose?"

"Er, no I don't think so." Riley had not included the incident at the shanty in his report because he hadn't wanted to be involved in the inquest. He had had no doubt that the sheer number of witnesses would have ensured that the investigating troopers would have received a factual account.

"Well you heard how he got young Johnny Cabel out at his old man's shanty?"

"Yes. I did hear something about that."

"That caused a bit of a stir. Not that anyone worried about young Johnny, but everyone's getting upset about this hanging business. Then on top of that Hatton held up the bank at Eurobin, shot the bank-manager through the leg, then went across the road to the police station, chased all the troopers away and set fire to the place—four prisoners inside too. Not that that mattered, they were only Chinese."

"He didn't hang anybody else?"

"No. Not this time. But he got away with something like four thousand pounds worth of gold from the bank, and that's upset 'em pretty badly in Sydney. That's why they called old Mad Mick down there. They want to know how Hatton held up a bank when there was a police station across the road and why the troopers ran away. I could bloody well tell 'em if it comes to that."

"Mm?" said Riley encouragingly.

"For exactly the same reason I'd run away if I'm sitting up with a bloody old carbine and half a dozen coves ride into town bloody well weighted down with breech loading rifles and these new American revolvers that'll kill a man at three hundred feet."

"Yes. I see your point," said Riley sympathetically: "And what happened to the Chinese?"

"The Chinese? Oh they fried," said the sergeant perfunctorily.

Riley collected the eight pounds that was left after the deductions from his pay and bade farewell to the barracks for another month.

And it was very nice to have eight pounds in your pockets, he reflected, as he rode through the dusk towards the Lightning Fork shanty. Eight pounds five as a matter of fact, because he hadn't spent all the two pounds he'd drawn the previous month.

Collingwood had told him there would probably be another dance on at the shanty. There usually was one every Saturday night during the summer. Riley had suggested that perhaps the dances might have been postponed for a time because of John Cabel's death, but Collingwood had not thought it likely. That they had not been postponed became evident when Riley was within half a mile of the place. The penetrating sounds of the fiddles carried far through the still evening air, and soon Riley could hear again the rhythmic crash of boots, and, a little later, the laughter and the voices.

At the shanty itself the scene was exactly as it had been on the evening three weeks before and Riley marvelled that death so crude and violent could have left so little mark. Most of these people must have been here the other night, he thought, and yet there didn't seem to be any restraint about their gaiety to-night. He would have thought witnessing something like the hanging would have kept most normal people away from the shanty for a year, or for good. But perhaps these were not normal people. Collingwood didn't think they were.

He studied their faces in the flickering lights of the lanterns and fires. Strange idea. Fires at this time of the year. Although probably their purpose was to keep the mosquitoes and moths away as much as anything else.

Not that it worked, he observed, slapping at something that was fluttering around his neck. The faces, he thought, taking up his theme again as he threaded his way through the drinkers in the yard making for the shanty door, were just faces. Highly coloured by the sun, and now, strangely lit by the yellow lights, perhaps, considered closely, they seemed somehow harsh and withdrawn. But then if you took any face, burned it under this sun, lit it with fire light, and then considered it closely, it might well look harsh and withdrawn. They were just faces. If he hadn't known that most of these men were sons of convicts . . . if he hadn't known that most of them had watched a hanging here three weeks before, he would have probably thought they were ordinary men. But then he did know.

The shanty itself was full of whirling couples, so full it seemed impossible that they could move. But the whole room was a mass of movement. The fiddlers were on their stand. He couldn't tell whether they were the same ones or not; but there was something massively absent from that shanty that night. The old man wasn't behind the bar.

It wasn't all that remarkable, thought Riley. There had been no logic behind his impression that one of the few permanent things in this world was old Dan Cabel's presence behind his bar. The noise was so great that Riley seemed to be moving inside it as he wriggled through to the corner of the bar, where a man in a white apron was drawing beer from a barrel.

Riley wondered whether perhaps old Dan Cabel had

sold the shanty and left. In that case Jane probably wouldn't be here either.

The man in the white apron looked at Riley inquiringly and he ordered whisky.

The man gave him beer and Riley said he'd wanted whisky.

The man smiled amiably and nodded. There was no hope of anybody hearing any spoken word until the dancing ended, so Riley paid for the beer and sipped at it.

Someone plucked at his arm and he turned and jumped so violently he spilled his beer when he found Jane Cabel at his elbow. She really was a very pretty girl, in her own wild way, was his first thought. What the hell did she want with him, was his second thought; had she recognised him without his beard after all? He almost raised a hand to touch the place where his beard had been.

She was speaking to him, but there was no earthly hope of hearing her. Riley smiled vaguely down at her. She was smiling at him, standing a little away from him in a peculiarly inviting manner. That was it, she was asking him to dance with her.

Riley smiled and shook his head, pointing towards his leg as though to indicate that he was lame. He had no intention of getting involved in that fracas that passed for a dance in the shanty, and he didn't want her to feel the revolver he was wearing under his coat.

Besides, he couldn't dance.

Nevertheless he didn't want her to get away. If this were a coincidence, it was a piece of good fortune for him and as such a most unusual thing, not to be treated lightly. If it was not a coincidence he wanted to find out more anyway. The thing was to keep her in conversation. How did you keep a strange woman in conversation under circumstances in which she couldn't hear a word said anyway?

Then suddenly the fiddles and the dancing stopped, just as Riley leaned forward to shout in Jane's ear: "Won't you have a drink?" which caused a burst of laughter in Riley's corner of the shanty. He heard someone shout, "Good on you, Janey!"

"Thank you, a half pint," said Janey.

She was wearing a long black skirt with a white high necked blouse with long sleeves which was perfectly decorous in itself, but which virtually forced upon Riley the conclusion that Janey was very prettily built. He wondered whether perhaps the black skirt was some local concession to mourning. Although there was nothing of mourning in the flushed lips and vivid eyes of the soft young face smiling up at him. Incredible that a girl like this could have been involved with a bushranger's gang. It was probably her brother more than herself. Careful Riley, there's no need to reach conclusions; just observe.

"You're Dermot Riley, aren't you?" she said.

Riley very nearly dropped his beer. His utter confusion was so apparent that there was no point in trying to hide his identity.

"I beg your pardon?" he said, foolishly.

"You're Dermot Riley aren't you, the man who nearly blew up Jimmy Hatton?"

She was talking quite loudly and Riley was frankly terrified that she'd been overhead. God alone knew how many bushrangers were amongst that mob now surging out of the shanty.

"You remember me," she said, laughing directly

into his face, but perfectly amiably Riley perceived in his anguish. "It was my face you slapped on top of the cave."

Why, grieved Riley silently, was he ever under the impression that he had any sort of control over his affairs. He was the merest wisp in the winds of fate. Still, there was nothing for this now but to put a brave face on it.

"Yes, Ma'am," he said smiling gallantly. "I remember you very clearly. I have never regretted any act more in my life."

"Oh that's all right," said Jane," you didn't hit me very hard. You had to do it anyway."

"That's a very tolerant point of view." He saw a shadow in her eyes and realised she didn't understand the word "tolerant". He could hardly explain it. Better just convey by his expression that it was complimentary.

"But why did you shave your beard, I hardly recognised you?"

Irresistibly, Riley's hand went up to his face. So much for the perfect disguise. What a waste of a thoroughly good beard.

"You were in the shanty earlier that day, weren't you?"

"Yes. As a matter of fact I was," said Riley, quite aware that there was nothing to be gained by any form of dissimulation.

"Pity you didn't blow that cave up on them. It was my fault wasn't it? I turned up at the wrong time, didn't I?"

Riley had seldom felt so at a loss in any conversation.

"Well now," he said, "I suppose it was a little

awkward." Why was the girl so extraordinarily open about her relationship with the bushrangers?

Her expression changed, by no means to sadness, but to a sort of reflective gravity.

"It's funny to think . . . but if I hadn't barged up there my brother Johnny would be alive today. Did you know they killed my brother?"

"Yes. I . . . had heard about it." Then she hadn't recognised him by her brother's body that night. But then that wasn't remarkable, the poor child would hardly have been in a condition to recognise anybody.

"Are you still trying to catch Jimmy Hatton?"

"Well now, I . . ."

"I hope you catch him," she said, dropping her voice and speaking fiercely through her teeth. "I hope you catch him and I hope they hang him. Want to watch 'em hang him and I want to dance on his grave."

Which no doubt were sentiments very proper to a recently bereaved sister, thought Riley, but he wished she wouldn't utter them so publicly. The shanty was by no means empty yet, and he had no wish to defend himself and this bush waif from the vengeful onslaughts of colleagues of James Hatton.

"Look," he said, "is there anywhere quiet here that we could talk?"

"Depends what you mean by talk," she said, raising an eyebrow at him.

"Oh no, I assure you, I simply mean talk," said Riley, embarrassed, but realising immediately that her coquettishness was purely automatic. This would be her stock reply to any man who asked her the same question.

"Come into the kitchen," she said, picked up her half pint of beer and led the way round the bar. Riley, following with his own pint of beer, heard a faint "Good on you, Jane" as he went through the hessian curtain. How many men, with less innocent intent than his own, he wondered, had been led into the kitchen. Not necessarily any of course, he told himself. These rough peasantish types were often coarse in their manners, but very restrained in their actual behaviour.

The kitchen was a small dark room, lit only by what light managed to filter through the hessian curtain. There was a heavy smell of meat and grease. Some dark shapes that were probably a table, a cutting block, some cupboards.

"There," said Jane, leaning against the table. "That's quieter isn't it?"

"Not appreciably," thought Riley, and it certainly wouldn't be when the dancing started again, however . . .

"Now look Miss Cabel . . ."

"Oh, why don't you call me Jane?" He could almost see her pouting. Just how automatic was this coquettishness?

"No, I think I had better call you Miss Cabel," said Riley gently, "It's an old Irish custom."

"Oh, are you Irish then. I wouldn't have thought so. My dad came from Ireland."

"How is your father by the way?" asked Riley, out of genuine curiosity.

"Oh, he's dead, didn't you hear? He died last week. Couldn't get over Johnny dying like that. Just grieved away, poor old Dad did."

"Oh, I'm sorry."

"Oh well, he was very old. What was it you wanted to talk to me about, eh?" She spoke distinctly invitingly.

This girl might reasonably be described as cold blooded, thought Riley, her brother murdered and her father dead of grief and her main interest seemed to be a flirtation with a stranger. Perhaps cold-blooded wasn't the word.

"I was just wondering," said Riley, "how serious you were about wanting to see James Hatton caught."

"I want that more than anything in the world," and Riley, hearing the deep loathing in her voice, believed her.

"Could you find out where he is for me?" he asked casually.

"Oh yes, easily," she said eagerly.

"How could you do that?"

"Oh I couldn't tell you how, I couldn't do that. But I could find out, really I could."

Why couldn't she tell him how? Actually there might be some reason in that; she'd be willing to betray the man but not the elaborate system through which he made his contacts. That would be the final disloyalty to the tableland people.

"All right, when?"

"I don't know. Soon. Where are you camping?"

"Oh I move about," said Riley vaguely, "I'll contact you here? When would you say?"

"Day after tomorrow. Monday?"

"Fine, I'll come back about this time."

"All right."

"Good, well I'll be off then."

"Oh no, stay and talk for a while."

"No thank you Miss Cabel, I'm sorry, but I must be off."

"Did she walk over to your horse with you?" said Collingwood.

"Yes," said Riley. "As a matter of fact she did. Why do you ask?"

"Then she knows where you're staying, or has a pretty fair idea."

"How?" said Riley, bewildered.

"She'd know the brand on the horse."

"Would she really?"

"Everybody within fifty miles of here knows the brands on my horses."

"Oh. And you think that's why she walked out with me, to find out?"

"No. She wouldn't have known then that you weren't riding a police horse. All I'm saying is that she certainly knows now."

"And do you think she's genuine?"

"She might be. It's very hard to tell. She's lying in one thing though, she certainly didn't recognise you."

"Then how did she know me?"

"Obviously if she didn't recognise you somebody must have told her."

"But how do you know she didn't recognise me?"

"Because, it was obvious, as you said, that she didn't recognise the man who was standing over her brother's body."

"But surely," said Riley reasonably, "under the strain of a moment like that . . ."

"Under the strain of a moment like that," said Collingwood, "the senses would be heightened to such a degree that even if she didn't recognise you at the moment she would remember having seen you as soon as she calmed down. She did neither. Obviously then she didn't know you at that time. She did later.

She hadn't seen you since, so someone must have told her. Really, you may be a brilliant tactical man but you're a bit weak on deduction. Here, have some more whisky."

"Yes," said Riley sadly, both to the observation and the invitation. He thought he'd been rather clever about the whole thing.

"Of course, none of this necessarily precludes her being genuine about wanting to see Hatton caught," he said.

"Exactly," said Collingwood. "You can't afford to ignore the situation, and you can't afford to act as though she were in absolute good faith."

"I wonder who could have told her who I was?"

"Could have been anybody," said Collingwood. "That's the trouble with this part of the world, it's impossible to keep anything quiet for more than a week."

Riley wished Collingwood had thought of that before he suggested he shave his beard off; he'd seemed much more confident of the soundness of the disguise then.

"Well," he said. "I suppose all I can do is go along with things and see how it turns out."

"Yes," said Collingwood, "but I'd be very careful when you go back to see Jane."

The shanty seemed inordinately quiet, ominously quiet in fact; although that was almost certainly only because there was no dance on. There was no-one at all in the yard, no horses outside. The only sign of life was the yellow square of light in the doorway. Be careful, Collingwood had said, but how did one be careful? He had to go into the shanty. If Jane had been laying a trap for him, entering the shanty was the most reckless thing he could do, so the idea of being careful was just a hopeful fiction.

Riley tethered his horse in the scrub a good hundred yards from the shanty. He had a breech loading rifle of Collingwood's in a saddle holster and he considered taking it with him. He would have liked to, but couldn't bring himself to walk through the door of the shanty with a rifle in his hands. He had two revolvers under his coat and they would have to do. They would probably be more than enough, he reflected wryly, to deal with one eighteen year old girl.

He hesitated outside the door of the shanty. Would it be feasible to call the girl out here? Feasible, but pointless. If there were men waiting for him they'd have their guns trained on him by now. And if they had any sense there'd be more of them posted in the scrub. Besides, the idea of standing out here in the night and bellowing "Janey" would make him feel altogether too foolish. Then at least it wouldn't be a bad idea to charge through the doorway, a revolver in each hand, ready to shoot should there be an ambush.

But how would he feel after such an entrance if all there was inside was one demure eighteen year old girl, and possibly one or two highly amused drinkers? No, there was simply nothing else for it. He had to go in as though he was utterly confident that Jane Cabel could be trusted; as he would have been if Collingwood hadn't raised doubts. Personally he was still quite convinced that Jane Cabel sincerely wanted to help him track down Hatton. In that case, he told himself, show the courage of your convictions and go on in.

Riley walked into the shanty.

The door slammed suddenly behind him and he knew before he turned round that he had been wrong . . . wrong, and incredibly foolish.

"Looking for me?" came the slow deep tones.

Slowly Riley turned. A fierce grin split Hatton's beard and Riley could see two perfect rows of huge white teeth.

Was this the way a man died, shot dead by this splendid looking bastard in a colonial shanty? At least Heaven send Hatton did use that revolver on him, God preserve him from any ghastly games with a rope.

Riley glanced around the shanty. It appeared to be empty apart from the two of them.

"Janey's not here if that's who you're looking for," said Hatton.

Riley didn't answer.

Hatton raised the fingers of his left hand to his mouth and gave a shrill whistle. There was an answering whistle from outside and in a moment the door opened and another man came in carrying a carbine. That would be the one who'd been posted in the scrub covering his arrival, thought Riley dispassionately. Odd how predictable it had all been, really. What a dreary, forlorn, stupid business. The newcomer shut the door after him. He was a short thick-set man with a heavy squint in one eye and a straggly ginger beard.

"Got 'im eh, Jim?" he said to Hatton.

"Got 'im," said Hatton.

He kept grinning at Riley, savouring as much as possible the triumph of capture.

"Listen," he said. "There's just one thing I want to know from you. It was Johnny Cabel told you about the plant up on the Ridge wasn't it?"

"Why do you ask?" said Riley.

"Just wouldn't like to think I'd hanged the wrong man," said Hatton.

A little late to worry about that now, thought Riley, but he'd better tell Hatton the truth in case he decided somebody else was the informer and dealt with him accordingly. After all he couldn't harm John Cabel any more.

"Yes," said Riley.

"Good," said Hatton, "Just see if he has any guns on him, Dave."

The squint eyed man approached Riley professionally and quickly found and took his two revolvers.

"Revolvers, eh?" said Hatton. "They starting to pay you traps a bit better now or did they give you blood money for poor old Mick Ramsden?"

Riley didn't answer. A deep lethargy had fallen on him. He didn't see any way out of this and he wanted it over quickly.

"Not a very talkative sort of cove are you?" said Hatton, laughing. "What do you think we ought to do, Dave?"

"Shoot him and get the hell out of here," said Dave quickly.

"No, I don't think we'll do that," said Hatton. "Shooting'd be very quick and easy wouldn't it?"

If they tried to hang him, thought Riley, he'd put up such a fight that they'd have to shoot him to keep him quiet.

"There might be others following him," said Dave quietly.

"No, I don't think so," said Hatton, "This is the man who works alone; this is the man who took on the whole lot of us on the Ridge all by himself."

The fact that he'd been single handed that night obviously had particularly rankled with Hatton, thought Riley, but at least he apparently admitted to himself and to his gang that there hadn't been a body of troopers involved.

"That was a filthy business, trying to bury us all alive," said Hatton, the grin snapping off his face.

Riley looked at him sourly.

"By God," said Hatton, "that might be an idea. What do you say we bury him up to his neck next to an ant heap?"

"No, Jimmy," said Dave, "let's get out of here. Shoot him and let's go."

"I won't shoot the bugger," said Hatton. "He'd have left us rotting under the ground up there until we suffocated or starved: I'm not going to let him out so quickly."

"Well hang him then if you want to," said Dave. "I'll go get a rope."

"Hanging's too quick," said Hatton.

"Well dammit, make up your mind," said Dave peevishly. He seemed to be listening for something.

"I think I'll knock him about a bit for a start. Here hold this," said Hatton, handing his revolver to Dave.

Riley watched the bearded giant walk towards him, saw the lips drawn back across the teeth, saw the fist slowly raised. Then a flash of red pain and he was reeling across the room, trying to suck the air back into his racked lungs.

"God what a reedy runt to have caused so much trouble," said Hatton contemptuously.

Riley blinked at the pair of them and decided he would make a dive for the squint eyed one and try to take his revolver. He would get shot, but that would put an end to this nonsense. How justified the sub-inspector had been in predicting that Riley would be the eighth special constable to die in the Goulburn district.

"I'll tell you what, bog trotter," said Hatton, "I'll give you a chance. We'll have a fight you and me, here in this shanty. You knock me out and I'll let you go. If I knock you out I'll wake you up and I'll gouge your eyeballs out and then I'll hang you." Hatton laughed loudly. "What do you say, want to try your luck?"

Riley ran his tongue around his lips. He couldn't speak yet.

"Come on, what do you say?" said Hatton: "Dave here'll see fair play, won't you, Dave?"

"Yes, yes all right," said Dave, "But get on with it. We haven't got all night."

"Well what do you say Irishman, want to put up a fight for your life?"

What did this maniac want, wondered Riley. Some sort of sport apparently, as a cat might want a live and defiant mouse rather than one supine and collapsed.

He nodded briefly. "All right."

"Good," roared Hatton, "Now then, Dave, you know the rules, we fight until one of us can't stand up. If it's me, let him go. If it's him—well I'll look after that."

He walked slowly across the room to Riley who stood quite still, breathing deeply. Hatton was some three inches taller than he was, twice as broad and could probably give him four or five stone. It was hard to tell how old he was, but he probably wasn't much older than Riley himself, and he seemed to be in iron condition. The outcome of this fight wasn't in doubt in anybody's mind, but if he could stay on his feet long enough something might happen. He might be able to snatch a revolver from Dave, or even make a break through the door.

Riley adopted a severely orthodox boxing pose, left arm and foot forward, right arm protecting his face and chest. As Hatton closed with him he flicked the left into the bearded face and caught with his right fist the heavy right handed blow Hatton threw at him. Then he was rolling on the ground in agony clutching at the searing burn of torn fibre in his groin where Hatton's heavy boot had sunk into the flesh.

Hatton stood over him and laughed.

"Can you get up?" he said, "Or can I start on your eyeballs now?"

Thank God, Hatton wanted his fun, thought Riley, as he dragged himself to his feet, or he could easily have finished him off then. But it didn't matter, he was coming in to do it now. Riley, still bending, felt rather than saw the boot rising from the floor towards his throat. He flopped to one side and the boot swung into the air so violently that Hatton almost fell over. Riley scrambled upright again and limped away backwards.

Hatton, grinning, followed him.

"Remember this?" he said, running a finger down the side of his face. The long scar was barely visible now. So he had been the rider on the path, thought Riley, no wonder he was enjoying this so much now.

Hatton made a sudden rush, both fists flailing low. Riley ducked, his head almost to the ground, swung away to one side striking out blindly with his right fist. It hit Hatton somewhere about the kidneys and he heard the man grunt.

Riley backed away again, massaging his groin to try to clear the crippling pain. Hatton was strong, incredibly strong, but he was also dead slow. Which probably only meant it would take him longer to kill Riley . . . but it mightn't.

Hatton was urging Riley back into a corner. He was advancing on him with his arms spread wide open to prevent his slipping by on either side. Riley stood straight up and waited for him, warily watching his feet. When he was about five feet away Riley suddenly lunged forward and smashed his fist hard on Hatton's nose. The big man bellowed and reeled back, the crimson already seeping down into his moustache in twin stains.

Riley saw him turn a furtive glance towards Dave who was standing by the door, revolver in hand. He hadn't liked even this minor humiliation in front of his henchman. The sudden hope that he might win this fight died in Riley as he realised that in any case they would never let him go. Hatton would never let any man live to boast that he'd bested him in circumstances like this. Still, he might as well do what he could.

Hatton was coming towards him again, more warily now, his own arms held up in something of a boxing posture. Riley waited, his left arm extended, ready to lunge in, strike and away again.

Hatton came in, throwing punches hard and regularly. Riley blocked and hit back but Hatton's fists struck into his ribs again and again. He backed away but Hatton followed rapidly, punching all the time. Then suddenly the man dropped to the ground and

Riley thought for one wild moment he'd knocked him down, but then he felt the massive legs scissored around his own and he was falling sideways to the floor.

This was the end, he'd never get out of this now. Hatton had his legs around his body, his feet locked, and Riley could feel the muscles swelling as he applied pressure.

Riley tried to throw himself over onto Hatton's body to break the lock, but the vast legs held him motionless and he could feel his bones giving under their strength. He could see Hatton's dark face, straining and grinning at the same time. Well damn the bloody man, there was only one possibility. Gasping for breath, Riley raised both fists in the air and smashed them down with all his strength into Hatton's groin.

The bushranger howled and his legs convulsively opened. Riley sprang free and Hatton rolled over once and stood up, his bloodied face glaring at Riley now with vicious hatred.

How much of this would he take, wondered Riley, before he grabbed the revolver again and took complete control of the situation. Probably quite a lot; once committed to a contest like this he wouldn't lightly admit himself beaten.

Hatton rushed him again, and Riley staggered under two savage blows to the head. He felt his lips crush and could taste his own blood. Falling he punched hard into Hatton's stomach, and then he saw the knee coming up. He swayed to one side, grabbed Hatton's leg in both hands and heaved. Hatton went over violently on his back. Riley moved round to try to kick him in the head, but the big arms were already poised, waiting.

Riley moved away and Hatton slowly stood up.

"Well," he said, breathing very heavily and wiping the blood away from his moustache and beard, "putting up quite a battle aren't you, bog trotter?"

He stood glaring at Riley.

"You know when I've gouged your eyeballs out I think I'll cut your tongue out before I hang you."

He probably would too, reflected Riley, who had a sudden vision of himself eyeless and tongueless, hanging from the rafter as John Cabel had done. No! He wouldn't. He'd kill this bloody bushranger with his bare hands first. Or make him kill him. He wouldn't be hanged. In fact damn and blast it all, he wouldn't die at all.

He walked suddenly towards Hatton, feinted at him with his right and kicked him full in the stomach. The big man bent double, like a snapped tree trunk, and Riley banged him on the back of his neck with his fist. Hatton's arms came out to grab him and Riley moved back and kicked him in the ear. Hatton almost went over, supporting himself on one hand and Riley went in again. He could see Hatton's swollen face was purple and he could hear the tremendous effort he was making to breathe. I've got him, thought Riley in exultation, I've got him, I'm going to knock him out. Hatton still had one hand on the ground, and Riley went round him cautiously then pulled his fist back and smashed it with all his force behind the bushranger's ear. At the same moment Hatton brought his right hand off the ground and swung it in a great sweeping blow which caught Riley full on the chest.

Both men sagged to the floor and sat down, their knees almost touching.

Just lift your foot and kick him, kick him in the face, Riley told himself as he stared at Hatton through a red haze, kick him in the face. But he couldn't move, he could hardly breathe, there was an unbearable roaring noise in his ears. He could see Hatton dimly now, the strong bearded face blotched and marred, and the eyes almost closed. The man was virtually unconscious. But so, Riley realised as he struggled to move, was he.

Slowly, terribly, infinitely slowly he pulled himself up onto his knees; then sagged forward again on to his hands. Detachedly he saw Hatton was trying to get up. He was getting up. He was on his knees. God damn you, Riley, stand up now or you'll never stand up again. But Hatton hadn't made it either. He was down on his hands too.

From a distance of three feet the two men, each on his hands and knees, stared balefully into each other's face.

Then, by unspoken consent, they backed away, slowly stood up, shaking their heads like old bulls who have fought too long and too hard. For the first time in some minutes Riley remembered the squint eyed bushranger. He looked round for him and saw him standing near the door, staring unbelievingly at the spectacle of his leader almost unable to stand. He had the revolver in his hand, but it was pointed toward the floor. As Riley watched, he took a tentative step towards Hatton.

"Eh, Jim," he said, "will I put a stop to this?"

"Keep out of it," grunted Hatton, "I'll finish this bastard off in a minute."

He came stalking across to Riley again, and Riley saw that he swayed a little as he walked. Riley waited where he was. Hatton made a half hearted attempt to kick him, then they closed, smashing leadenly into each other, virtually taking turns to hit. Neither of them made any attempt at defence, they had no strength for that.

Hatton's blows had stopped hurting Riley. Each time one landed now there was just a new area of numbness. One of his eyes was closed and there seemed to be a lot of blood in the other one. Dimly he knew that Hatton could take this much longer than he could. He knew he was hitting Hatton, by the jarring in his own arms, but he didn't know where. He couldn't stand up much longer like this.

He fell back, knuckling at his eyes to try to clear them of blood. He bumped into something. His back was against the wall.

Hatton paused and looked at him. Riley saw him gathering himself and knew he was going to charge in with one immense finishing effort.

He was coming, trundling almost at a run, his arms already swinging. No hope of surviving this. Can't go back. Do something different, do the unexpected; the last desperate gamble.

Riley dived headfirst at Hatton's feet, rolling himself into a ball as he went.

Hatton tripped over him and fell full length. Riley leaped up and jumped onto Hatton's back. He kicked him in the back of the head so that his face smashed into the floor. Hatton rolled over. Riley kicked him under the chin, twice. Hatton groped out with one feeble arm and Riley kicked him on the elbow. Then, he smashed the heel of his boot into his face. Hatton lay back, quite slowly. Riley kicked him in the head. He stood back and raised his boot again. If he kicked him enough he would kill him.

"That's all," the squint eyed bushranger, revolver ready, was walking towards him. "That's enough. Get away from him.'

And this was it. Now he was shot simply and quickly dead. But play the thing out for what it was worth.

"All right," he said, breathing heavily: "I think the bargain was that I could go now."

Limping so much he almost fell each time he took a step, Riley moved across to the doorway. He expected the bullet in his back any moment, but he didn't much care. His mind had only strength enough for one concern, and that was forcing his body to stay upright until he reached that door. If he were shot that put an end to the matter, but until then he would concentrate all his being on just reaching that door. Something seemed wrong deep inside him. He felt as though he had a cold iron bar set somewhere in his bowels and his body, from the waist down. seemed to be a jellied mass of pain.

He couldn't see the squint eyed bushranger. But he knew he was standing over Hatton, puzzledly looking after Riley, wondering whether to shoot. If Hatton recovered before he reached the door he would be dead, Riley knew. It didn't matter. Even if they called on him to stop he wouldn't. They could shoot him. There was a chance this way. And if this failed there was nothing else he could do. But he must stay on his feet. If he fell down now he'd never be able to get up again.

Suddenly he was at the door.

Painfully he stretched out a hand and raised the latch. This was the moment. The shot would come now if it were going to come at all. Slowly the door swung open and Riley limped out into the night.

God, he'd forgotten- his horse was a hundred yards away. Hatton would come to long before he reached it at this rate.

He broke into a shambling run. The pain washed all over him but soon he became used to it. It was only pain. Once he fell over, but was back on his feet before he realised he couldn't do it. His horse snorted and started as he reeled up to it and he had a bad moment with the reins in his trembling hands. There was the carbine in the saddle holster. Dimly it occurred to him that he could go back and try to shoot both bushrangers. He would have a reasonable chance. But a much more reasonable chance of falling unconscious before he reached the shanty. A point he proved by fainting in the saddle as the horse cantered off down the road.

He realised later that he couldn't have been conscious for more than half that ride, and when he finally dismounted outside the homeyard at Collingwood's station, he sagged to the ground and passed out again.

CHAPTER SIX

"DON'T BOTHER TRYING TO tell me what happened," Collingwood was saying. "Just tell me whether you think anybody's following you."

Riley felt the firm texture underneath his hand and knew he was lying on the carpet in Collingwood's living room. There was a cushion under his head.

Collingwood was giving him whisky. The woman who did the cooking was hovering anxiously.

"I don't know," he said, "I don't think so. I'll be all right in a minute." In fact as long as he didn't try to move, he didn't feel all that badly. He was aware, more than anything else, of being very glad to be alive.

He sat up.

"I'm all right," he said. He stood up. Then he sat down again, abruptly, on the floor.

"Leg's stiffening," he said explanatorily.

"We'd better get you to bed," said Collingwood, grabbing him under the arm pits.

"No! Not at all," said Riley. "Just give me a hand into that chair." Collingwood and the woman lugged him into the chair.

Riley took a deep drink of the whisky. He felt much better.

The housekeeper went off to get him some food, and Riley told Collingwood more or less what had happened.

"My God," said Collingwood at the end. "You're a lucky man."

"Yes. I suppose I am really. A fool though; I should never have walked into that."

"Mm," said Collingwood non-committally, but implying that he agreed. Which was rather hard, Riley thought vaguely. After all Collingwood, directly and indirectly, had been substantially the organising force behind the whole affair.

"Anyhow," Collingwood said, "I'd say we're almost certain to see more of Mr. Hatton tonight.' '

"What, out here?"

"Depends how badly you hurt him; but he's going to hate you like hell now. You've done the worst thing you can do to a man like that—you've made a fool of him."

Riley thought about that for a moment. It seemed to him that Hatton had previously disliked him sufficiently to execute him, so any added disfavour he may have incurred wasn't all that important.

"I must say," said Collingwood, chuckling, "I wish I'd been there."

Perhaps, some time, a long time from now, thought Riley, he would be able to look on that night in the light of a stimulating adventure. But just now it was too close, and death had seemed too real a possibility. He was beginning to think he wasn't cut out to be a special constable. But then he had never really thought he was.

"I'd better get the men up," said Collingwood. "Would you like to go to bed for a while. I'll wake you up when the excitement starts—if it starts."

"No. I'll be all right," said Riley, "but how likely do you think it is they'll turn up here tonight?"

"Can't be sure, of course," said Collingwood cheerfully, "but I'd say quite likely. You see Janey will have told 'em you were riding one of my horses. They won't know you're here of course, but they'll think it's possible and they'll be thinking it's about time they had another try for Cicero anyway. I'd say there was a very reasonable chance we might see some sport here tonight. Jimmy Hatton will be very anxious to see you dead."

"All right," said Riley resignedly leaning back in the chair, "You go and wake some men up. I'm sorry about this incidentally. I wouldn't have come back here if I'd thought they'd follow me."

"Rubbish," said Collingwood, "they'd have come

here anyway. Besides I don't mind. In fact I rather like this sort of thing occasionally. Sure you wouldn't like to lie down for a while?"

"Quite sure thanks."

Collingwood went off to rouse his men. Riley put his whisky down on the arm of the chair and tentatively stood up. His head was aching badly, but otherwise he seemed much better. He tried walking and found that he limped very heavily on his right leg. He sat down again as the housekeeper came in with some mutton chops.

"Now this is the way I've worked things out," said Collingwood, spreading a rough drawing of the house on the table in front of Riley: "We've got eight men and yourself and me. I'm putting a man in each room on the outside of the house. That gives us two men on each side. Each of them has a rifle and a revolver and plenty of ammunition, and I'm setting up a reserve of guns and ammunition in the hall where anybody can get at it. What do you think of that?"

"Seems admirable," Riley said, smiling at the eager face of his host. There was a sudden commotion and clatter at the rear of the house.

"Don't worry, they're just bringing in the horses," said Collingwood.

"Horses?" said Riley.

"Just Cicero and Barnstorm," said Collingwood: "They're the only blood stock I have on the place at the moment. We've turned the rest loose in the lower paddock. Hatton won't worry about them. That's one thing you can be sure of in this country; if your horse is not absolutely the best no bushranger will touch it."

"I see," said Riley, wondering just where the horses were to be stabled.

"This of course leaves the men's quarters completely undefended," said Collingwood, bending to his plan again. "But there's nothing we can do about that. Hatton will probably realise that at once and make that the base for his attack—which won't do us any harm because there's a hundred yards of clear ground between us and there."

"What did they do last time they were here? said Riley.

"Last time, they just surrounded the house and kept firing," said Collingwood. "But that was different. They were only interested in keeping us inside while they got off with the horses. This time they'll be attacking the house to get at you."

"Of course," said Riley uncomfortably.

"In fact," said Collingwood," our great danger, if they realise it, are these." He pointed to a number of shaded areas on his plan. "Those are the shrubs in the house garden. If they've got the common sense to work up behind those they can get very close to the house—which will give them a chance to set fire to it—which is what I presume they'll try to do."

It struck Riley that what Collingwood was doing was deducing what he would do if he were in Hatton's place. Which was quite a reasonable point of view, although it argued a peculiarly violent trait in Collingwood himself.

"Of course they won't necessarily come," he put in mildly.

"No. No. I realise that," said Collingwood impatiently, "but it won't hurt to be prepared."

"But there is this," persisted Riley, "if they do, it

mightn't be a bad scheme for me to let them see me then take off for Goulburn. If you lent me a decent horse it's not likely they'd catch me, and it might save a lot of trouble."

"Well of course you can do that if you like," said Collingwood, a little haughtily, "but I wouldn't advise it."

"Just as you like," said Riley soothingly, "it's just that this isn't exactly in line with your original plan of leading them here, I mean you haven't had time to prepare for them properly."

"Oh we'll make out." And with a wave of his hand, Collingwood dismissed any further theoretical objections.

"Now as far as these shrubs are concerned," he said, pointing to his plan again. "I suggest that you and I make it our business to put a few bullets through each of them every five minutes or so, whether we can see anybody or not . . . what do you think?"

"All right. It'll use up a lot of ammunition.

"Oh we have any amount of ammunition," said Collingwood.

"Then it's an excellent idea."

"Now I've had the dogs tied up all around the verandahs. They'll bark the place down as soon as anyone comes within a mile, and they'll be useful for the close work as well."

Riley nodded intelligently. He was feeling very tired, and this battle of Collingwood's seemed a very remote affair.

"We've plenty of water and food in the house, although I don't imagine they'll lay siege for long. We've got about four hours to dawn, but there's a good moon which is to our advantage. On the whole

I think that's about the best we can do. What do you think?"

Riley did his best to think. He felt he should make some intelligent comment on the whole affairs. But then he knew very little about defending homesteads from bushrangers; he doubted that there would be any necessity to anyway, and he was feeling exhausted.

He nodded silently.

Collingwood was standing over him expectantly.

"I think you've worked things out very nicely," Riley said at last.

"Nothing you want to add to it?" said Collingwood.

Riley thought again, desperately.

"Have you made any provision for dealing with the wounded, if we have any?" he said on an inspiration.

"Good man," said Collingwood, as though he'd come up with something brilliant. "I'll see to that. I'll set out some bandages for Mrs. Andrews." He strode out of the room, and Riley thankfully sank back into his chair.

"Dermot Riley, Dermot Riley," he murmured. "You're a long way from home." All of this dramatic activity, all the violence he'd seen and taken part in the past few weeks seemed to him to be in some way quite apart from himself. He was not of this land nor of these people. No matter how deeply he became involved, as on the Lightning Fork Ridge, or in the shanty that night, he was still, essentially a spectactor. And when the time came, as seemed very likely, that this land or these people finally killed him, he would die, in a sense, as a spectator, half accidentally involved in an affair that was none of his business.

Yet curiously he had a deepening conviction that his destiny was linked with James Hatton; that there was between himself and this man whom he scarcely knew a widening area of antipathy that would have to be resolved. James Hatton, he knew, hated him, and with reason; whereas he, through a series of involuntary mental, or emotional process, had come to regard Hatton as the embodiment of everything that was loathsome about Colonial life. And so he was too, if it came to that. But what he disliked about him most was the theatrical quality he brought to all his actions; the sickening, boring flamboyance of the man, that led him to hang people, and hold mock trials and force Riley to fight for his life. That was the most unlovely aspect of Hatton, Riley thought, as sleep began to weave strange and comforting shapes in his brain. His public assertion as virtues of what were childish, vicious, perverted vices. And he was so damned good looking too. That was unforgiveable . . . the great, blundering bag of loathsome matter.

Riley wasn't sure whether he was dreaming or not when he started to think about Jane Cabel. She must have left him and gone straight off to Hatton to tell him how Riley could be caught. A great judge of character, Dermot Riley, you're a great judge of character. But how had she recognised him anyway? Simply enough, really. Someone from the station might have been at the shanty, or someone from the Goulburn barracks; they knew who he was. Should have thought of that before. But it was strange that he had been so wrong about Janey. A pretty girl too. Oh, a great judge of character Dermot Riley, a great judge of character.

He sat up suddenly in the chair, aware that he had been briefly asleep. Collingwood was in the room and two men. They were talking.

"Well I can't make you of course," Collingwood said, "but I think you're being completely unreasonable."

"Can't see it, Mr. Collingwood," said one of the men, a thick-set hairy man of about forty. "We're paid to look after sheep, not fight bushrangers."

"Besides," said the other man, a younger battered looking fellow, "we've got no quarrel with Jimmy Hatton. If he's out after your friend here——" gesturing at Riley—"well that's between the two of them. Got nothing to do with us."

Collingwood ran his fingers through his hair in exasperation.

"Well what do you propose to do?" he said: "Just ride out into the night?"

"We'll go into Goulburn," said the older man. "We'll tell the troopers you're expecting trouble if you like."

"That'll be a great deal of help," said Collingwood heavily: "They're likely to turn out for anybody on the tablelands who expects trouble."

"I'm sorry, Mr. Collingwood," said the younger man, "but I'm a married man. I got to think of me family."

"Yes, yes, yes," said Collingwood impatiently.

"Anyhow, there's no point in trying to persuade you to stay if you don't want to."

"We'll be back in the morning," said the older man.

"Oh, I don't know that I'd bother about that," said Collingwood coldly.

"You mean you're sacking us?" said the old man.

"Well that's not the way I would have put it," said Collingwood. "I would have said you were walking out on me."

"But there'll be no jobs for us tomorrow, is that it?" said the man belligerently.

"Since at this stage we don't even know whether there'll be a homestead here tomorrow there seems little point in discussing the matter further," said Collingwood.

The younger man stepped forward a little.

"Now hold on," he said. "I want to get this straight. Are you telling us that we either stay here and risk our skins to save your mate's neck here, or you sack us—is that it?"

"I see no necessity to discuss the matter further now," said Collingwood. "If you're going I suggest you go."

"All right," said the younger man, "all right, Mr. Colling-bloody-wood, we'll go. But we won't go by ourselves. Come on, Jack." The two men walked out of the room, a sense of injustice evident in the very set of their shoulders.

"Colling-bloody-wood," murmured Riley. "Remarkable."

"Colonials," said Collingwood disparagingly. "Rer.arkable people."

"I don't know that I altogether blame them," said Riley. "It is after all none of their affair. It's none of yours really, if it comes to that."

"Don't be so damned tolerant," said Collingwood snappishly: "I'd better go and see what's going on out there."

He came back five minutes later and slumped down in a chair opposite Riley.

"Well we've got four men left," he said: "Our two friends raised the banner of unity and two of the others have gone off with them."

"That hardly leaves enough to defend the home-stead, does it?" asked Riley.

"Depends how many men Hatton brings, and whether or not anyone here gets hurt," said Collingwood: "Anyhow, it's all we've got so we might as well make the best of it."

The idea that the bushrangers were going to make an attack on the homestead had become an established fact in Collingwood's mind, Riley realised. He thought of pointing out that it wasn't necessarily the case, but decided that to do so would only increase Collingwood's irritability.

"You and I will have to keep moving round from room to room," Collingwood said." Do you feel up to that?"

"Surely," said Riley, who didn't.

"We'll only have one man on each side of the house, but we should be able to give the impression that there's more. Anyhow, do you feel like coming for a walk around and I'll show you how I've got things set out?"

"Of course," said Riley, draining his whisky and levering himself out of the chair. He found that provided he walked very slowly and leaned on anything handy to take the weight off his right leg he could make reasonable progress. His head had stopped aching he discovered, shaking it gently to make sure.

Collingwood led him on a tour of the house. The front rooms were held by a youth whose age Riley estimated at around sixteen. He was sitting next to the window clutching a vast revolving rifle.

"Be careful of the recoil on that thing." said Collingwood. "Sure you wouldn't be happier with a revolver?"

"No. I like this, Mr. Collingwood," said the youth. "Anyway I've got a revolver here as well."

"All right. Don't forget to blow that lantern out as soon as anything happens. You don't want to be looking out that window with a light behind you."

"No. I won't forget, Mr. Collingwood."

"All right, Dave. Keep your head down."

"Yes, Mr. Collingwood."

Collingwood and Riley moved round to the western wing. "Good boy that Dave," said Collingwood.

"Bit young for this sort of thing, isn't he?" said Riley.

"Do him good. Anyway, he likes it," said Collingwood, who, Riley felt, was inclined to attribute to other people what he considered the proper sentiments.

The western wing was held by a competent looking middle aged station hand who already had his lantern out, and was standing by the window with a revolver in his hand.

"Like a drink, Bill?" Collingwood asked.

"Wouldn't mind, Mr. Collingwood."

"I'll send Mrs. Andrews in with something.'

Riley peered out the window. He could see the black bulk of the men's quarters outside the home yard.

"Give a shout if you hear anything," said Collingwood to the station hand, and to Riley: "Come and we'll have a word with Charlie.

They passed the kitchen on the way to the back rooms and Riley heard horses hooves moving on the stone floor. He supposed that was as good a place as any to keep horses in a house.

Charlie, charged with defending the rear of the building was a full blooded Chinaman, whom Riley recognised as the men's cook. He was armed with a shot-gun and had two revolvers laid out on a chair near the window. He seemed very sleepy and not particularly interested in the events of the night. He spoke politely enough in what to Riley, who had never seen a Chinaman before he came to Australia, was a quite incomprehensible accent.

A lean elderly man answering to the name of Andy was standing by the window of the room in the eastern wing which Riley used as a bedroom. He was inclined to disparage the whole idea of a raid.

"They'll never come now, Mr. Collingwood," he said, "it's too close to dawn. They'll allow 'emselves more 'n a few hours to take this place."

"You might be right, Andy," said Collingwood, "but it won't hurt us to make sure. Have you got everything you want in here?"

"Everything except a drop o' rum."

"Well I think that might be fixed. Don't forget to put that lantern out if any shooting starts."

On their way back to the main living room, Riley and Collingwood passed Mrs. Andrews in the hall laying out rolls of bandages on a side-board. Several open boxes of ammunition were stacked in the centre of the hall where they could be most easily reached from any part of the house. Riley noticed that there were still plenty of weapons in the arms rack. Apart from a formidable deficiency of numbers, he thought, they were quite well equipped to withstand a siege. His sword, he observed was still on the peg where he'd hung it the first day he came to the station. Riley wondered fleetingly whether he would ever use it again.

Collingwood sent Mrs. Andrews round with rum for the men and a cordial for the boy.

"He'd probably prefer rum," he said, "but I don't

147

think I ought to encourage him. Well now, what next?"

All that was required, thought Riley, was bushrangers, and he was becoming increasingly convinced that there weren't going to be any. But then, he admitted to himself, his convictions were usually wrong, so he'd wait and see.

"You might as well try to have a nap," said Collingwood, "I'll call you if anything happens. I'll just go for a wander round. By the way you'd better arm yourself hadn't you?"

"Eh?" Riley said.

"You'd better take a revolver from the rack hadn't you?"

"Oh yes, of course." said Riley, who hadn't realised he was the only man on the premises not armed.

Collingwood grinned at him, the first real evidence of humanity he'd given for some time.

"I sometimes wonder whether this is altogether your line of country."

"So do I," said Riley, "So do I."

Then, two loaded revolvers in his belt, he sank back into his chair and fell asleep while Collingwood prowled restlessly round the house.

The dogs were barking. Riley stirred in his chair. The dogs were barking. Riley sat upright suddenly. The dogs were actually barking. They were barking frantically.

Collingwood came running into the room.

"They're here," he said excitedly: "Out behind the men's quarters, I think." He went round the lanterns in the room, blowing them out.

Riley stood up slowly and shook his head.

Collingwood turned the last of the lanterns down, leaving only a faint glow of light.

How predictable these blasted bushrangers were, thought Riley, how predictable to anybody but himself. He took a couple of steps and found his leg was much stiffer than before, but not so painful.

"How many are there?" he asked stupidly.

"No idea," said Collingwood, "but you can be sure there's a lot of them. They wouldn't try a thing like this without an army behind them."

There was the sound of a shot from the back of the house, then an answering fusillade from outside. The dogs became frenzied. Collingwood drew back the curtains from one of the windows and peered out into the night. He had a revolver in his hand and he thrust it forward out the window, but didn't fire.

Riley went across and looked over his shoulder. The gardens looked very peaceful in the moonlight, the shrubs throwing long, very black shadows. The shooting had stopped now.

Riley saw a movement in one of the shadows thrown by the shrubs, or thought he did.

"Is there somebody behind that bush near the gate?" he whispered.

"Which one?"

"The tall one, near the fence."

"Put a bullet into it," said Collingwood.

Riley took out his revolver and fired. The sound was very loud and sharp in the room. The smell of powder hung vividly in the air. There was no movement in the shrub.

Collingwood fired two shots himself. Still nothing happened. Then a series of shots came from the other side of the house, outside, but very close.

"Come on," said Collingwood and led the way out of the room.

Mrs. Andrews was sitting in a chair in the hall. She had a shaded lantern on the floor. She seemed quite calm, but didn't say anything as they went past. Riley took a handful of ammunition from one of the boxes and put it in his pocket.

The boy Dave was kneeling by the window, his rifle balanced on the still. He looked round as they came in.

"See anything Dave?" said Collingwood.

"No Mr. Collingwood. I think they're all round on the other side." There was a dog just outside the window barking furiously.

"They're in the men's quarters," said Collingwood, "almost certainly. Come on."

The room held by Bill, the middle aged station hand, was already thick with smoke.

A shaft of moonlight through the window showed it hanging heavily in the air.

"A mob of them just came up from the back paddock," said Bill, without preamble. "Six or seven I think and I reckon there must have been halfa dozen of them there already."

There was a burst of gun fire from the men's quarters. Riley could hear the bullets thudding into the outer walls of the house. One came through the window and hit high up on the wall, bringing down a cloud of plaster.

Bill thrust his revolver out the window and fired five quick shots. There was another shot from outside and one of the dogs was hit. It howls rose high above the barking of the rest. Then it quietened down, suddenly.

Bill had reloaded his revolver and now he took up a rifle.

"They haven't got a hope of getting near the house on this side without being seen," he said, "but God help us if they try to rush us."

"We'd stop them," said Collingwood. "Three of us can bring a lot of fire to bear."

As if to illustrate his point he stood at the window and emptied both his revolvers at the men's quarters. A tremendous volley came in return and Riley could see the flashes of the guns from the shadows of the building. Several bullets came in the window this time and a water jug behind Riley shattered.

Collingwood was kneeling below the window, reloading. Riley, feeling rather diffident, and not at all anxious to expose himself, stood by the window and quickly emptied his revolvers. It seemed pointless to him. He knew how difficult he found it to hit anything he could actually see. This pouring of shots into the night seemed wasteful. But presumably it made the bushrangers keep their distance. He knelt down to reload and Bill took over the window with his rifle. Bill, Riley observed, knelt while he fired, and allowed no more than his eyes to appear above the window at one corner. Much more sensible than standing and exposing most of the body.

The heavy blast of a shot-gun sounded inside the house, then the lighter crack of a revolver.

"I'll go and see," said Riley. "You stay here."

He assumed the shot-gun had been fired by the Chinaman and he found him standing by the window firing intently into the night obviously at some target.

"What is it?" said Riley.

The Chinaman said something Riley couldn't understand. Riley stood by his shoulder and looked out the window. He saw a point of flame flare near the fence bordering the home yard. Then he heard the shot and at the same time felt a tearing sensation in his coat. There was someone out there, near the fence. He could see the bulk of a man.

The Chinaman's revolver clicked empty and he picked up another one and started firing again. Riley tried to aim through the window, but he found he couldn't line up his sights.

The man out in the yard fired again. The bullet struck the wall near the window.

"You'd better kneel down," Riley said to the Chinaman, who was standing squarely in front of the window so that he was exposed to the waist. The Chinaman took no notice but fired steadily until his revolver emptied. Then he moved away from the window, picked up his shot-gun and began to reload it. Riley knelt and thrust his revolver out the window. He still couldn't sight the man, but he fired five quick shots in his general direction. The man fired again and Riley heard the bullet come in the window. It hit something wooden behind him.

The Chinaman was lucky he wasn't standing there then, thought Riley. Then he was aware that the Chinaman was behind him, leaning over him with the shot-gun. The blast of the gun deafened Riley, and left his ears ringing.

The shadow near the fence became suddenly elongated. The man was running. Riley fired at him. He could see him quite clearly now in the moonlight, running along beside the fence around towards the men's quarters. Riley fired again remembering now to aim a couple of feet in front of the running figure. He fired again, leaning forward out the window. The man kept running. He would be round the corner of the building soon. There was a burst of shots from the other side of the house and Riley saw the man waver. Then an answering volley from the paddocks. Riley fired his last two shots as the man ran out of the line of sight. A dog was barking very close to him and Riley realised he was hanging almost out the window. He pulled back inside the room.

The Chinaman was chattering away excitedly and grinning all over his face. Riley couldn't understand him, but he clapped him on the shoulder and grinned back.

He went back to where he left Collingwood. Mrs. Andrews was still sitting placidly in the hall. She had her hands folded on her lap. Riley smiled at her as he scooped up another handful of cartridges. She smiled back. Remarkable woman, he thought. Collingwood greeted him with: "We should be shooting up those shrubs. We will in a minute, but just look here."

Riley looked out towards the men's quarters. He could see the glow of a fire, but not the fire itself. It was as though someone had started a blaze out of sight around the corner of the building.

"What do you make of that?" said Collingwood.

The silhouette of a man passed briefly across the glow and Collingwood snapped a shot at him.

"I don't know," said Riley. "But I do know that if they surround the place and come in on all sides at once we haven't a hope of stopping them."

"Well, let's hope they don't think of that," said Collingwood: "Look at this. They must be mad."

Three moving flames appeared from behind the men's quarters and were floating erratically towards the homestead. It took Riley several seconds to realise that they were torches being carried by men. At the same time a fusilade of shots thudded against the walls of the homestead. The dogs barking hit a new crescendo of frenzy.

The station hand's rifle exploded harshly and Riley saw one of the flames drop to the ground. He couldn't see the man who'd been carrying it. The other two flames came on towards the homestead.

"Mad," muttered Collingwood, "absolutely mad." He was firing his revolvers deliberately.

"Don't aim at the flames," he said. "Aim about two feet below them."

Riley stood beside Collingwood at the window. The station hand was kneeling in front of them. All three fired simultaneously. The leading flame dropped to the earth as though it had been thrown. In its light Riley saw the body of a man. The flame seemed to be burning his head.

The third torch was still coming. Two or three bullets rushed through the window near Riley's head and he wished he could move out of range. He could see the man carrying the third torch quite clearly now. He was only twenty yards from the house. Why did he keep coming? He must know he had no chance.

As though the man had suddenly realised just that he stopped and flung the torch towards the verandah, turned and fled back towards the men's quarters. Collingwood and the station hand both fired at him, but he kept running. Riley watched the torches slow arc through the air. It fell harmlessly on to grass, a few feet from the verandah. All three torches were stll burning, marking a crooked path from the homestead to the men's quarters.

"That's one of them done for," said Collingwood. "He hasn't moved."

"What about the first one?" Riley said. "What happened to him?"

"I don't know. I never saw him. I think he must have dropped the torch and ran. What on earth did they try that for?

He didn't seem to expect an answer. Riley stared out the window at the figure of the man lying on the ground with the flames at his head, like a halo. He wondered whether any bullet he had fired had found its way into that body. Was this the second man he had killed? Odd how this sort of thing carried with it so little emotion apart from the excitement. Or was there a certain amount of joy in it; was this pleasure he felt as he smelt the biting fumes of gunpowder and looked out into the night where the enemy lay concealed? He rather thought it was.

"Come on," said Collingwood. "Let's go and flush out those shrubs."

Riley went with him through to the living room and they stood at the window and conscientiously pumped bullets into the unresisting shrubs. Nothing happened.

"Still," said Collingwood, "it won't hurt to let them know we have that approach in mind. Not that they're likely to be any trouble if they come carrying torches every time."

"If I was doing this," said Riley, "I'd be inclined to make a sort of mine out of a gun powder barrel and ride up to the house with it."

"That won't occur to them," said Collingwood confidently. "These people aren't very imaginative."

"How long do you think they'll keep this up?"

"God knows. Not after dawn anyway, I shouldn't

think. Still that gives them plenty of time. It's not two o'clock yet."

The shooting had stopped altogether now and even the dogs began to quieten down. Riley and Collingwood walked round the house. The youth Dave wanted to leave his post and move to the side of the house facing the men's quarters.

"I haven't fired a shot, yet, Mr. Collingwood," he pleaded. "No-one's going to come in this way."

"You stay where you are," said Collingwood. "You'll get all the shooting you want before the night's out."

The old station hand, Andy, they found trying to stem the flow of blood from a wound in his cheek. Only one bullet had come in his window and it had grazed him. Collingwood sent him through to Mrs. Andrews to get the wound bandaged.

"It's just as well they don't know how many people we've got in here," Riley said," or they mightn't be so reluctant to rush us."

"They'll rush us eventually." said Collingwood. "That's all they can do. Obviously they know there's no point in just staying out there firing at the house. They might have another try at setting us on fire—but I think they might be discouraged about that. No. They'll rush us. The trouble is that once they get on the verandah there's not much we can do about it. Except of course that they've still got to get inside."

Andy came back with most of his face swathed in an amateurish bandage.

"Lot of bloody good this is," he said disgustedly.

"It's alright Andy," said Collingwood. "Keep your head down next time."

They heard the Chinaman's shot-gun, the first shot for some time, then the rapid fire of a revolver. More distantly the sound of shots from outside, and men shouting.

They found the Chinaman at his window firing steadily.

He said something to Collingwood who joined him at the window, firing out towards a twinkling line of flashes that came from the fence. There must have been half a dozen men shooting from out there. There wasn't room for Riley at the window and he stood back waiting for one of the others to run out of ammunition. Bullets were hitting the outside wall with staccato rapidity and several came in the window. Some actually passed between Collingwood and the Chinaman. Another dog was hit outside. It didn't yelp. It just stopped barking suddenly, and then Riley could hear its feet scrabbling on the boards. Then it was still.

The heavy crack of a rifle came from the front of the house. That must be the boy shooting.

"They're coming on both sides," shouted Collingwood. "Go through and help Dave."

Riley, wincing at the sudden pain in his leg as he tried to run, stumbled through into the front room. Dave was firing the rifle through the window.

"They're in the garden," he yelled. "Lots of them, in the garden."

Riley knelt at the window beside the boy. He saw a man run from the front fence and dive behind a shrub. He fired twice at the base of the shrub. He thought he heard a yell. Then a figure crawled from behind the bush on hands and knees, making back towards the fence. Riley fired again. The figure flopped forward on its belly. It was still moving towards the fence. Riley fired again. The man lay still, another shadow on the shadow laced lawn.

Riley reloaded while he sought another target. A man jumped from behind a bush and ran towards the far corner of the house. Riley fired at him. The men kept running. He disappeared around the corner. Riley heard a shot from the other side of the house.

Someone leaped out of the garden and ran at the house, straight towards the window.

Dave fired his rifle twice. The running man doubled over and sprawled full length near the verandah. Riley saw one of the two dogs tied on the verandah straining towards the body.

"I got 'im. I got 'im," shouted the boy, "did you see that? I got 'im."

There were two shots, very close, on the verandah, just outside the window.

Riley realised, as though it was some separate phenomenum, that both the dogs out there were suddenly silent. He heard a scraping of boots on board. Someone was on the verandah. Within feet of them.

Riley thrust his hand out the window and fired five shots quickly.

A hand appeared from below the window on the outside and fired twice into the room.

Dave fired at the hand from a distance of about six inches, but seemed to miss.

Riley thrust his revolver over the window still and fired downwards twice. He wanted to fire more, but didn't want both his revolvers empty, not with someone outside so close. He reloaded quickly, while Dave stood a little back from the window, ready to shoot.

The wall shook with a sudden series of crashes. Someone was hacking at the front door with an axe.

"Stay here," Riley shouted to the boy, and ran through to the front hall.

The axe head was already splintering through the panelling.

Riley waited until it was pulled out and then fired through the hole. Someone cursed outside and several shots were fired. No bullets came through the door. Riley fired through the hole again. He heard footsteps outside on the verandah. Then a shout and three shots from the room Dave was in.

Riley ran back, unconscious now of the pain in his leg. Dave was half-lying on the floor, the rifle in his hands pointed at the window.

"I'm all right," he said. He wasn't. Riley could see the stain low on his left side even in the dim light.

A man appeared at the window and Dave fired. The man disappeared. The crashing against the front door started again.

A vivid awareness that this battle might be lost struck Riley for the first time. He ran back to the front door and fired through the widening hole. Half a dozen shots answered him, the bullets chopping into the wall near him. Incongruously he thought of Mrs. Andrews sitting in the hall around the corner. Were her hands still placidly folded?

There seemed to be shooting coming from all sides of the house now, but they were getting in here.

"The front door!" yelled Riley: "The front door's down!" but he doubted whether anyone could hear him.

One of his revolvers clicked empty. The door was half gone now and he could see the man with the axe. He fired at him and heard the man grunt. He fell away from the door. But then the axe started its battering again. Riley couldn't see anybody wielding it. He ran up to the door, thrust his revolver through the hole and fired, once, twice, three times. The revolver was empty.

He fell back into the hall, fumbling with cartridges. There wasn't time for this. He got two into the chambers, pointed the revolver at the disintegrating door and pulled the trigger. He had to pull it three times before the cartridges in the chambers worked round to the firing pin. Two shots and then it was empty again.

The door was down. Men were forcing their way into the house. They were shooting. Riley felt a thud in his right leg. His revolvers were empty. He threw them at the men. The gun rack. It was next to him. He clutched at it; a rifle to use as a club. His hand fell on his sword and he sobbed harshly as he pulled it clear of the scabbard.

A man was pointing a revolver at him. Riley slashed at the man's arm, felt the sword bite in deep. The hall seemed full of men now. Riley charged into them, flailing with the sword. There were shouts. A gun fired twice. Something struck him in the face. He felt the sword crash on somebody's head. A pair of hands were clutching at his legs. He was trampling on a body. There was a flash as a shot was fired. Riley saw a dark face, mouth open, eyes glaring. He thrust with the sword, thrust with all his weight. The point hit something, was resisted, then slid in deep. Someone screamed. The sword was stuck. Riley dragged it clear, held it double handed, smashed into the tangle of bodies in the hall.

Someone was shooting again. Behind him.

"Down Riley, down!" someone was yelling That's the way he used to speak to a dog he once had, he thought absurdly.

The flash of a gun near his face. He swiped at the flash with his sword. He missed. The sword swung down and struck something soft on the ground.

"Get down Riley you bloody fool!" More shots behind him. That was Collingwood. He suddenly saw what was wanted and fell to his hands and knees so that Collingwood could shoot over him.

Two hands closed round his throat and he felt himself being pulled to the floor. He dropped his sword and groped till he found a face. He couldn't breathe. There was a biting pain in his throat. He gouged at the face, seeking eyes with his finger nails. Teeth bit hard on his fingers. He wrenched them free.

There was a lot of shooting behind him, above him. He shoved himself forward butting his head savagely into the face of whoever was throttling him. The hands left his throat and he felt a body pulling away from under him. Someone kicked him hard in the chest.

There were more shots. Someone screamed.

Then suddenly it was quiet.

Someone was pulling him to his feet. It was Collingwood.

'Quick," he was saying, " back here. I've got to get that sideboard in the doorway."

Riley stood up. He was surprised to find he could. He didn't seem hurt at all, although his leg was wet. He put a hand down. It came away sticky. He must have been shot. It couldn't be much.

Collingwood was struggling with a sideboard. Riley went to help him and together they shoved the heavy bulk into the doorway.

"That'll hold 'em," said Collingwood. "God that was close."

The shooting had stopped altogether now. Only one

dog was barking. The rest were probably dead, thought Riley.

"Dave's shot," he said.

"Oh God, is he indeed?" said Collingwood, going into the room the boy was holding without waiting for an answer. Riley followed him. Dave was still lying against the wall with the rifle in his hands. "I'm all right," he said.

Collingwood lit a lantern, shaded it with a floor rug, and knelt down to examine the boy. Riley stood by the window and looked out into the yard. It seemed quiet.

"I don't think it's too bad, Dave," said Collingwood after a while: "I think it might have chipped one of your ribs, I don't think it touched your lungs. Can you breathe alright?"

'Yeah," said the boy, "Hurts a bit though."

"That could be the ribs," said Collingwood, "Just lie there boy. We'll get a doctor out to you in the morning."

"Hadn't we better take him through into the hall?" said Riley.

"Good idea," said Collingwood, "Mrs. Andrews can put a bandage on him. Give me a hand would you?" Riley and Collingwood picked up the protesting boy and carried him through into the hall. Mrs. Andrews clucked when she saw him and began tenderly taking off his shirt.

Riley went around to the arms rack and found himself two more revolvers. As an afterthought he took two more as well, loaded the lot and thrust them into his belt.

He found Collingwood standing over Mrs. Andrews

as she bandaged the boy. He had a bottle of rum in his hands.

"I think a drink all round, don't you?" he said.

"Mr. Collingwood," said Dave.

"Yes, Dave?"

"Do you think I could have rum this time?"

Collingwood laughed. "I think so boy, just this once."

Riley went around with him as he called on the defenders of the homestead and filled their glasses with rum.

"I suppose I could have left them with a bottle each," Collingwood said, "but they'd all get drunk as lords and then where would we be?"

Where indeed, Riley thought.

He remembered his leg and looked at it in the dim light of the hallway. He'd been shot in the top of the thigh. The bullet had passed cleanly through. It wasn't bleeding much. It was a very shallow wound, just under the skin.

"What happened then?" he said to Collingwood: "Did they come in on your side too?"

"No. That was just a cover for the others. Just as well. We'd never have stopped them if they had."

"They must be getting sick of this," said Riley: "I know Dave and I killed two of them and I think I must have hurt some in the hall. Did you get any?"

"No. Don't think so. But I'd say there must be anything up to twenty men out there or there were."

"I didn't think Hatton worked with a gang anything like that size," said Riley.

"He has done. They say he had nearly thirty when he held up the Mail at Crookwell last year. A lot of them are part timers. He calls on them when he wants them. That's probably why he took so long getting here tonight. Gathering his forces."

"What's in it for them?"

"He's probably spun them some yarn. Or more likely they've been in robberies with him at some time or other and daren't refuse."

"I feel that I'm more trouble than I'm worth," said Riley reflectively.

"Nonsense," said Collingwood briskly. "There's nothing lost so far."

"What if that boy dies?" said Riley softly so that Dave wouldn't hear.

"He won't," said Collingwood confidently. "Come on let's take another look around."

Everything was so quiet now that it seemed the bushrangers might have left. But the one remaining dog was still straining on its lead and growling, and they could see the glow of the fire behind the men's quarters. It showed no signs of diminishing.

"How would it be," said Riley, "If I slipped out and came up on the other side of them? If I made enough noise they might think I was a force of troopers."

"Possible," said Collingwood, "but not worth the risk. If we lost you we'd never hold the homestead."

You wouldn't need to, Riley thought, but didn't say anything. He was feeling acutely aware of the fact that too many peoples' lives were being risked to protect him. Admittedly it had been at Collingwood's insistence, but still . . .

"You'd better take Dave's place in the front room," said Collingwood: "I'll keep wandering about for a while. Keep on shooting at those shrubs. They know they can get close to the house that way now."

Riley pulled a chair over by the window and sat where

he could look out over most of the home garden. He could see the body of a man Dave had shot, and further away, near the fence, a shadow that he thought was the man he had killed.

The whole business would be farcical, if it weren't so bloody, he thought. Somewhere out in that moonlight night was the tall, bearded deep voiced bushranger whom men knew as James Hatton, marshalling a body of men to attack the homestead for the express purpose of capturing or killing himself, Dermot Riley. And here was this body of men, willing to be killed, apparently, to satisfy the lust for revenge of James Hatton. Who were these people who would turn out at night to do bloody murder at the call of a man like Hatton?

A situation very akin to high farce, he thought. And he smiled as he lay his revolver barrel on the window sill so that it glinted in the moonlight, because, for himself, he had to admit that he rather liked it.

"Oh Paddy Malone," he sang softly.

"Will you ever go home?"

"'Twas the thief of an agent, that caused you to roam."

And somewhere, somehow, sometime, he would again come face to face with James Hatton. Eventually one of them would kill the other, he knew as surely as he knew that one day, if he lived, he would leave this sunlit country and return to the mists and rain of his own cloud wrapped island. The two beliefs stemmed from the same type of intuition, except that one was borne of hatred and the other of regret. But he would meet Hatton again, possibly even this night, and one of them would die. Hatton he hoped.

Riley saw the shape of a man stealing very slowly, very close to the ground, along by the fence near the gate to the homestead garden. He appeared to be carrying something.

Very calmly Riley raised his revolver, steadied it on his arm and lined the sights up on the slowly moving shadow.

"I am about to kill a man," he thought, deliberately. He felt nothing except a certain cold amusement.

He fired. The man dropped and writhed. Riley fired again. The man lay still. That was all there was to it. A man could become very competent at this sort of thing, Riley thought, wonderingly, as he reloaded. A scattered volley in reply to his shots came from over by the men's quarters, but soon died away.

Collingwood came hurrying into the room. Riley told him what had happened.

"By God we'll discourage them at this rate," said Collingwood: "What was he up to do you think?"

"I don't know. He was carrying something. He might have been going to try to set fire to the place. One man would have a much better chance than a bunch of them."

"It'll be light in an hour," said Collingwood, "if they're going to try anything else they'll try it soon."

There was a sudden crackle of concentrated gun fire from the other side of the house. "Old Andy's side," said Collingwood and ran out. Riley limped after him.

The room seemed to be full of flying bullets. They were coming through the window and smashing into the plaster wall. Andy lay dead on the floor. A shaft of moonlight fell on his face. He'd been hit in the head at least three times. The bandage he'd had on his face had been almost shot away.

There was a flare of light somewhere outside, but

the bullets rushing through the window were almost visible. It was impossilbe to look out. At least ten men must have been pouring a constant stream of shots into the room.

"Next room," said Collingwood.

Bullets were coming in here too. But not many. Riley and Collingwood knelt at the window and peered out. A burning cart was being trundled across the yard towards the house. It was blazing fiercely. It looked as though it had been loaded with great heaps of flames. Somebody must be pushing it. There must be men at the shafts on the other side. But it was impossible to them through the flames.

Collingwood emptied a revolver at the cart and the stream of bullets from outside was immediately directed to their window.

"No good," said Collingwood, crouching below the window. "We can't stop them from here. What the hell now?"

"Water," said Riley. "We'll need water. Is there any in the house?"

"Not enough," said Collingwood: "Kitchen tank. Not enough. I should have thought of that. God damn it."

Riley dug his knuckles into his forehead in a desperate effort to think. The rush of the bullets above his head and their crashing into the wall behind him seemed to disorientate his mind. And the flickering increasing light in the room that meant the cart was getting closer. If it hit the house they were finished. It had to be stopped somehow. How far away was it? Fifty yards and moving fairly slowly. With a sudden access of clarity he told himself, almost calmly—when the situation is impossible the only course is the out-rageous.

"Don't shoot me," he called to Collingwood, and scuttled out of the room on his hands and knees.

The front way would be best. He ran through the hall. Mrs. Andrews was holding Dave's hand. Damn it, he'd forgotten the front door was blocked. He turned into the living room and scrambled out a window. Keep low. Round to the side of the house. He had to get between the cart and the house. Nobody behind that blaze would be able to see him. As long as nobody shot him from the house. He was running along the verandah. Strange, his leg didn't hurt at all now. He tripped over something. It was the body of a dog. His revolvers! He pulled two out of his belt. They were loaded, weren't they? Yes, he hadn't fired them since he'd loaded them. There was the cart now. It seemed to be stuck. No. It was moving again. Down low, close in along the verandah. Get between the cart and the gun fire.

The air was full of bullets. Of course, they were shooting at the house. Keep low. Keep low, below the level of the windows. They can't see you.

Everything seemed to be happening terribly slowly. He was almost detached from himself, watching from a distance as he picked up one leg after the other, with such immense deliberation, with such ponderous effort. And yet he was moving faster than he'd ever moved in his life before. He knew he was. He must be.

There was a shot from just behind him. Dear God, don't let them shoot from the house. That would be too much, to be killed by his own people.

Now, out to the cart. Bend almost double. Run as you've never run before. What if his leg gave in? What if he fell in the path of the cart and couldn't get up again? He wouldn't fall. He'd get there. The outrageous always worked. Remember how he'd cut back to the cave on Lightning Fork Ridge. Remember how he'd thrown himself at Hatton's feet as the bushranger moved in to kill him. When had that been? A month ago? A week ago? God! Only that same night, only a few hours ago.

His heart was bursting. It was taking so long to cover the ground. And yet it was only seconds since he'd left Collingwood. Only seconds. But he was only halfway to the cart. It was so light. Surely they could see him. But no. Remember they were behind the flames. They wouldn't be able to see past the flames.

Now he was almost there. What was he going to do? He'd had a plan, but what had it been? He could only remember that he had to reach the cart. Well, he'd reached it, dear God, and what now?

Riley ran in close to the cart, so close that the flames seared him. He saw a man pushing on one shaft and shot him as he ran. Shot him in the stomach because that was a target he couldn't miss. The man fell. The shaft of the cart dropped to the ground and the cart lurched to one side. There was the other man, gaping at him, holding the shaft with one hand, his face all lit and ruddy in the firelight. He was trying to pull out a revolver. Riley shot him in the body and again in the head. He saw the man's face shatter and he fell over backwards as though somebody had hit him hard and suddenly with a hammer.

The cart. Tip the cart over so nobody else could push it to the house. Riley grabbed one of the shafts and heaved. The crackle of the flames was fantastically loud. It wasn't the flames. It was gunfire. Bullets were thick around him. They were hitting the cart and the ground around his feet. One hit the shaft between his hands. Riley heaved and the cart tilted. He got a shoulder under the shaft and heaved again. One wheel was well off the ground. One more heave would do it. There was something moving in the cart. There were barrels in the cart. Small barrels. God, it was gunpowder! How long before it went off? Time enough to tip the cart, surely. The barrels weren't burning. Riley heaved again and the cart went over.

He dived around the cart again. Get between the flames and the men with guns. He was running back to the house. But his feet took so long to reach the ground. He had to wait until they landed before he could move them again. God, don't let anyone shoot from the house. But he was on the verandah. It had been as quick as that. He made a long dive for the nearest window and went in head first. He hit the floor and heard the bullets smacking into the wall beyond him. He lay there, breathing so hard each breath was almost a scream. But he'd done it. He'd done it.

The room suddenly filled with light. There was a long hissing boom from outside. The gunpowder had gone up It hadn't exploded because it hadn't been compressed. It had just burned out suddenly. In the glare he saw Collingwood standing in the doorway, grinning at him.

"You're not hurt, Riley, tell me you're not hurt, man!"

Grateful words, but he couldn't speak, not yet. He could hardly breathe. Whisky, that was what he wanted, whisky. But how to tell Collingwood, he couldn't speak.

Slowly his breath came back and he crawled out of

the room. Leaning on the older man he went into the hallway, grabbed a bottle of whisky, pulled out the cork and drank long and deeply, as though it was water.

Nothing had happened for almost an hour. The dog outside was quiet now. The moon had gone but there was a pre-dawn glow over the countryside. Nothing moved.

Collingwood thrust his head out the living room window.

"I wouldn't do that," said Riley.

"I think it's all over," said Collingwood: "I think they've gone."

He came back into the room and turned up the lantern.

"I wish you wouldn't do that," said Riley, whose chair was in line with the window and who was too tired to move."

Collingwood laughed. "They've gone. They would have shot me then if they hadn't. The dog's quiet. They've gone."

Collingwood looked as though he'd just had a refreshing night's sleep, thought Riley. The man's eyes were bright, his cheeks glowed above the fringe of neatly shaped beard. Riley ran a hand over his own stubble-covered face. He might look and feel better if he hadn't started this wretched shaving nonsense. The sky was shot now with the lances of dawn and Riley realised he could see a long way across the paddocks.

"I'm going to take a look around outside," said Collingwood.

"Not yet," said Riley. "Wait for a while."

"No. I'm sure they've gone. Don't you worry, sit there and rest," Collingwood said, making for the door.

"Wait on! Wait on," said Riley resignedly, and heaved himself out of the chair. His whole body felt like one massive ache and his right leg was so stiff he could barely bend it.

They went out through the hall where Mrs. Andrews was fast asleep in her chair, still holding the hand of Dave, who semed to be asleep too. Riley looked worriedly at the boy's white, strained face.

Collingwood went on ahead and warned the station hand and the Chinaman, then he and Riley went quietly out through the back door and stood on the verandah. Riley half expected to hear the crack of a rifle, but he was too tired to care much. The sun had slipped a red rim over the horizon now, and it was quite light. Some kookaburras in a clump of trees just outside the home garden set up their spasmodic clatter. A dog, some sort of half-bred coursing hound, was straining at its lead, whimpering with pleasure, trying to reach Collingwood. Another dog of the same type lay dead beside it.

Collingwood slipped the leash from the dog's collar and it bounded delightedly around them for a moment then loped off towards the men's quarters. Riley and Collingwood watched it silently. It disappeared behind the building, then came out on the other side, its nose to the ground, its tail lashing.

"It's all right," said Collingwood. "There's no-one there." The dog found the body of a man near the home garden fence and began sniffing at it cautiously. Collingwood whistled it and it came back obediently. He tied it to the verandah again.

The two men walked slowly across the dew-wet grass towards the men's quarters.

The body the dog had found lay just inside the home garden fence. It lay on its face, one hand still holding the torch which was now a charred stick. Most of the hair on the man's head had been burned away.

Riley looked morosely down on the body. The fact that it was lying in the wet grass seemed to make it particularly dead. The man had been quite young. Riley had no inclination to turn the body over. He led Collingwood away towards the men's quarters. They found the remains of the fire and the ground all round the building was littered with spent cartridge cases.

At the back of the building a man was sitting leaning against the wall. The front of his shirt was heavily stained with blood. He looked as though he were asleep. his head nodding down on to his chest. But he had to be dead. He was a short, fat, bearded man, and he looked very relaxed sitting against the shed in the dawn light.

Riley walked up to the body and saw a wide cut in the front of the shirt which seemed to be the source of most of the blood. This must have been the man he stabbed in the hall. He must have dragged himself back here then quietly bled to death while the battle went on without him.

My God, thought Riley, how many men did I kill last night? He found the killings rested very lightly on his mind. It was reasonable that they should, but it was surprising just the same.

"We'll have to get all these bodies into Goulburn some time today," said Collingwood.

That was going to be a remarkable entrance, thought Riley, envisaging himself driving a dray loaded with corpses. He was feeling lightheaded now.

The men's quarters had not been broken into. They were bullet-scarred, but hadn't been damaged at all otherwise, except where the wall had been scorched by the fire.

They walked back towards the front of the house. All the white wooden walls were marked with black splotches where bullets had hit. Around the windows the splotches ran together to form great black scars. Collingwood waved to the station hand who was standing at the window with a rifle in his hand. He pointed downwards to two dogs lying under the window.

"One's still breathing," he called. "Will I shoot him?"

"Yes," shouted Collingwood.

The shot sounded very thin and sharp. The dog didn't move.

There were two more dead dogs on the front verandah. One was lying with its head on its paws, its eyes open, staring towards the body of a man lying doubled up near the verandah.

"That's the one young Dave shot," said Riley. It was the body of a big, bearded man, and Riley thought for one moment it was Hatton. But it wasn't. A revolver was lying near the man's head. A few yards away they found an axe. It had blood on the handle.

There was another body near the gate to the homestead garden. It was doubled over a small barrel of tar. One side of its face was turned up to the sky, and one eye stared blindly into the morning sun. He had been a young man, too, no more than twenty-five. An ill-fed, stupid face.

"He must have been going to try to light that tar and throw it at the house," said Riley.

"Yes," said Collingwood, who seemed finally subdued at this concrete evidence of the slaughter that had taken place in the night.

Riley had expected to find another body here. He'd

shot a man behind a shrub and shot him again as he crawled away. He'd seen him fall and lie still. But there was no other body.

They went round to the other side of the house where a great patch of grass had been seared black by the burning gunpowder. The cart had burned to ashes. There was only one body here, the man he'd shot twice. The other man, shot in the stomach, must have crawled away, or been dragged away. But he must have been alive—they wouldn't have bothered taking away a body. Riley thought of a man with a bullet in his stomach out in the scrub in a bushrangers' camp. He wouldn't live long, poor devil; people rarely did live long with stomach wounds, even with the best of care. Riley wished he'd killed him outright. He didn't mind killing men who were trying to kill him, but he recoiled from the thought of a man he'd shot dying slowly, in pain, taking days to die perhaps.

A few crows were flapping around above the lower paddocks, blacker than ever against the flaming morning sky. Their cries were harsh and ominous.

"We'd better get these bodies into a shed," said Collingwood.

"Yes," said Riley. He kicked morosely at a trail of black ants weaving across the ground.

"I'll get Bill to take Dave into a doctor straight away," said Collingwood. He was speaking abstractedly, as though his mind was on other things. They stood in silence few moments longer, then on a mutual impulse turned and began walking back to the house.

"What about old Andy," said Riley, "did he have any family?"

"A sister, I think," said Collingwood. "She lives in Goulburn. I'll go and see her this afternoon.'

They walked on in silence a few more yards. "A bad business," said Collingwood, "a bad business."

"Yes," said Riley, wondering whether on the scale of infinite values Andy could be said to have died for him. Probably not. He hadn't thought the bushrangers would come. He had been wrong about that. So had Riley.

"I must get some more dogs while we're in Goulburn," said Collingwood.

"Yes," said Riley.

CHAPTER SEVEN

THE MAGISTRATE'S FACE was very red and he mopped at his brow with a large handkerchief. He spoke very quietly, so quietly that the sombre ticking of the vast clock hung high on the wall of the courtroom could be heard punctuating his voice.

"It is then the verdict of this court," he said, "that James Henderson, John Crew, Sydney Mounsey, David Prior and Brian Davies were shot dead while committing a felony at the Brinda station on the night of November the 16th, this year, and that therefore the shooting of these men fall into the category of justifiable homicide.

"Inasmuch as two of the deceased, James Henderson and John Crew, were proclaimed outlaws, I propose to recommend to the Reward board that the rewards offered for the capture dead or alive of these men be distributed amongst the defenders of the Brinda homestead on that night and among the relatives and dependents of those who were killed in the defence of the homestead."

He paused and mopped at his face. The clock ticked

loudly. Riley could hear the heavy breathing of the spectators in the gallery of the courtroom. One man cleared his throat and several others immediately did the same. They sounded like people in church during a pause in the sermon.

"It is further the verdict of this court," the magistrate continued softly, "that Andrew Hickey and David Simpson were murdered at Brinda homestead on that same evening by one James Hatton, proclaimed outlaw, and by other persons unknown; Andrew Hickey by being shot dead and David Simpson by having wounds inflicted from which he died."

Riley had a sudden vision of the boy Dave lying white and silent, his hand in Mrs. Andrews. 'From having wounds inflicted from which he died,' seemed a slender epitaph.

"It only remains for me," said the magistrate with no alteration in the volume or expression of his voice, "to express my own admiration and the admiration of the community at large for the courage and determination of the men who, at Brinda homestead, defied and inflicted such heavy losses on the members of the Hatton gang. I must particularly express my admiration for the deeds of the special constable Dermot Riley, who by his valiant disregard of self appears to have been largely responsible for preventing the outlaws overwhelming the homestead."

Someone was sobbing loudly at the back of the court. If I had never come to Australia, thought Riley, Dave and Andy would be alive now. Or would they? Were things as complete as life and death contingent upon chance to such an extent? Would Dave and Andy have died anyway? If not by a bullet, by disease, by a horse's hoof, by any one of the thousand possible accidents that beset the path of any man. Was he, Dermot Riley, simply one of several alternative links in a chain of events that would have inevitably sent Dave and Andy into eternity? Anyhow it was not a problem he was likely to solve in a hurry.

"Something must also be said," went on the magistrate, "of the devotion and loyalty of the employees of the station who resisted—in the case of two of them, resisted to death—the attack on the property of their employer."

What of the four men who had left before the attack started, wondered Riley. Were they ashamed now that they were not included in this accolade? Probably not. They were probably glad they were not in the company of Dave and Andy, already mouldering in their graves in the hot soil of the Goulburn cemetery. And he wasn't sure that their point of view was unreasonable. He wasn't sure that it mightn't have been better if they all, Collingwood himself, Dave, Andy and the others, had evacuated the homestead as soon as they thought there was a chance they might be attacked. Many people would then have been alive who were now dead. Or would they? That was the same point as before. Why bother with it? The dead were dead!

"If all the people of this colony," said the magistrate," reacted to the bushrangers with the same bravery and constancy as these people of Brinda station, the scourge of outlawry which wracks the colony would vanish overnight."

Three men at a table just in front of the semithrone arrangement at which the magistrate sat were scribbling furiously on sheets of papers. It was just as well they could hear what was being said, Riley thought, because he was sure the people in the gallery couldn't. But then it sounded as though the magistrate was speaking specifically for the newspaper men. "Scourge of outlawry," would look well in those headings of larger than usual type with which the newspapers introduced their accounts of various happenings. Riley had become very familiar with newspapers and their employees of late. The defence of the homestead had excited the interest of all the newspapers in the colony. One, *The Burrangong Miner,* had even had a ballad composed which it featured prominently on its front page. Riley had read the ballad until he came to a line in which Dermot Riley was rhymed with "standing firm not slyly." He had put the paper away with a shudder.

The magistrate had finished speaking and was gathering up his papers. The police, the newspaper men, the officials and the spectators, straggled to their feet. The magistrate walked briskly out of the courtroom.

"Let's go and have some beer," said Collingwood, who'd sat next to Riley throughout the hearing.

"Yes," said Riley.

"I wonder how much is involved in those rewards?" said Collingwood as they stood at the bar looking out through the glare of the doorway into the dusty, busy main street of Goulburn.

"Mm," said Riley, whose thoughts had been straying in the same direction.

"Probably no more than two hundred pounds for each man," said Collingwood. "They weren't particularly notorious. I'd never heard of them."

"Still, that's four hundred pounds," Riley said.

"Yes," said Collingwood. "We'd better arrange for it all to go to old Andy's sister. There doesn't seem to be anybody connected with Dave."

"That would probably would be best," said Riley in non-committal tones. He wished he had the same automatic generous instincts as Collingwood. He agreed with the principle of all the money going to Andy's sister, but he could not help a faint twinge of regret. Of course, his ungenerous self whispered before it was suppressed, Collingwood was in a position to afford to be automatically generous. For Heaven's sake, he told himself, searching his mind to make sure he wouldn't really have the money distributed any other way, and reassuring himself by finding that he would not, for Heaven's sake. Just the same he sometimes wished Collingwood wouldn't treat him so consistently as a gentleman amateur.

There was the sound of heavy feet on the boards of the hotel verandah and the doorway was darkened by a bulky figure. The sun outside was so bright that the man's features were obliterated, although Riley distinguished the trooper uniform. The man strode across to Riley and Collingwood, and he was quite close before Riley recognised him as the Sergeant who'd once acted as his warder.

The trooper touched his finger to his cap.

"Afternoon, Mr. Collingwood," he said, then turned to Riley: "The sub-inspector's back. He wants to see you urgently."

"Madden?" said Riley.

"Yes," said the trooper. "He's back!"

"Oh," said Riley, who'd nurtured an irrational hope that he might never see the sub-inspector again.

"He said *urgently*," said the trooper.

"All right," said Riley wearily. "I'll go."

"How long is he likely to be?" said Collingwood.

"I've no idea, sir," the trooper replied.

"I'll see you back at the homestead then," Collingwood said to Riley. "I'm still a couple of dogs short, and there's a fellow got some for sale I want to see."

The trooper knocked on the door of the sub-inspector's office and opened it tentatively. "Special Constable Riley's here, sir," he said.

"Send him in, send him in," said the sub-inspector and his voice held the note of geniality which Riley now knew boded only ill.

He walked into the office. Involuntarily he stopped just inside the door. He knew he shouldn't stand and gape. He knew that was just what the sub-inspector had expected, and wanted. But he couldn't help it. This was the most improbable thing in all this improbable colony.

Jane Cabel was sitting in a chair in front of the sub-inspector's desk.

"Come in Riley, come in," said the sub-inspector heartily. "Don't just stand there."

Jane had looked up once and smiled slightly and shyly at Riley. Now she was looking into her lap where she held her hands folded. She was wearing a high necked black dress which hung in folds around the chair. Riley took a few more shaken steps into the room and stood before the desk, just a couple of feet away from the girl.

"You know Miss Cabel, don't you?" said the sub-inspector.

"We've met," said Riley.

"Yes, well that's all right then," said the sub-inspector. Riley found himself looking anxiously for the fleck of foam on the sub-inspector's beard. It was there, just below his lip on that small tuft of hair that sprouts centrally just above the main growth on the chin.

"I see you've taken your beard off," said the sub-inspector and Riley wondered, as he had done before, whether this man had some capacity for reading, or at least connecting in some way with other people's thoughts.

"Yes, sir," he said carefully. "I did it to preserve my *incongeeto* as you suggested."

No flicker of irritation marred the horrible merriment of the sub-inspector's face, and Riley knew that he was to be allowed his shaft unscathed.

"Quite the fancy man now, isn't he, Miss Cabel?" said the sub-inspector, who was leaning expansively back in his chair. Soon, Riley knew, he would lean forward on to his desk and start making his point.

Jane looked up hastily and a suggestion of a smile appeared on her lips. She was a pretty jade, thought Riley in spite of himself.

"And you've been covering yourself with glory while I've been away," continued the sub-inspector. "Showing us, old regulars, how to do it, eh?"

Riley made a deprecatory gesture.

"I suppose you'll be rich now with all your reward money, eh?"

Riley tried to answer with a half smile, but the sub-inspector leaned forward a little in his chair and said, belligerently, "Eh?"

"Yes, sir," said Riley.

The sub-inspector leaned back again and smiled. At least, thought Riley, it was to be supposed he was smiling. His mouth was stretched wide over his yellow uneven teeth, and Riley could see a suggestion of yellow tongue. It wouldn't have been considered a smile in any other face, but it was probably the best the sub-inspector could do.

Abruptly the sub-inspector leaned forward onto his desk and cupped his face in his hands. Here it comes, thought Riley, here it comes.

"Now you'll be pleased to hear that you're to have another chance to show what you can do."

Riley could see it coming; some peculiarly unpleasant and dangerous assignment.

"Miss Cabel here has given us some very valuable information as to the whereabouts of James Hatton."

Curious the way the man's speech so often lapsed into formality, thought Riley, as his mind struggled to take in what had been said.

He looked at Jane, but her eyes were cast down.

"In fact, Miss Cabel has told us where James Hatton is—where we can find him." The sub-inspector brought this out triumphantly and sat waiting for Riley to reply.

"I see, sir," said Riley, after a moment. He knew what was coming. He couldn't believe it but he knew it was coming.

"And I have decided, Riley, in view of your . . ." he paused, searching for a word — "in view of your record, to give you the opportunity of making the capture."

Riley stared into the man's pig face. It could not be true. This could not happen to him. But he had felt that way before in this man's presence.

"Now," said the sub-inspector, leaning back in his chair, "do you know Dead Horse Marsh?"

"No, sir," said Riley promptly.

"No," said the sub-inspector smiling. "I didn't think you would, being a stranger to the country, so I'm having a little map made up for you. It'll be ready before you go. Anyhow that's where Hatton is, and that's where he'll be for the next week, Miss Cabel tells us. He's got a *plant* in the marsh and he's resting up there with a couple of wounded men. That's how Miss Cabel came to know where he was. She was, ah, approached with a request to supply bandages and ointments for the wounded."

This had gone far enough, thought Riley.

"Would it be possible for me to speak to you alone for a moment, sir?"

The sub-inspector looked at him solemnly.

"Is it about this business, Riley?"

"Yes, sir."

"Then I don't think it's necessary for us to be alone, Miss Cabel is, after all, vitally concerned. Besides, I think I know what you're going to say."

Riley stared at him in numb wonderment.

"Very well, sir. You've read my report on my last encounter with Hatton?"

"Of course, Riley, fully. Very interesting I found it. A little highly coloured, perhaps, but then we can forgive that."

"Then you will remember," persisted Riley, "that I said that Jane Cabel deliberately led me into a situation which very nearly ended in Hatton killing me?"

"Yes, Riley, I read that. But you jumped too hastily to conclusions, young fellow." The sub-inspector in an avuncular mood was intolerable, thought Riley. "Miss Cabel has explained all that to me. She didn't know Hatton was going to be there that night. It was just one of those unfortunate coincidences. No, no, Riley,

I'm quite confident that we can rely completely on Miss Cabel's good faith."

"Well I'm afraid, sir . . ."

"If I am confident of Miss Cabel's good faith," said the sub-inspector, menacing again now, " you may be confident too. It's me who makes the decisions around here, Riley, not you. It doesn't matter what the papers might say—you're still just a special constable, which means you've got about as much say around here as a blacktracker. Is that quite clear?"

"Yes, sir," said Riley. It was no use. Reason was useless with the irrational.

"Your orders then are to proceed to Dead Horse Marsh and capture or kill James Hatton."

"Single handed, sir?" said Riley almost sarcastically.

"No, no!" said the sub-inspector, genial again now. "You mustn't think us unreasonable. We don't want a valuable man like you killed. What would the papers have to write about if you weren't with us? No, Riley, we're not sending you out against Hatton alone."

Riley looked at him warily. It was too much to hope that he was to be given a force of armed and trained troopers. That would be too reasonable. That would give him half a chance in the obvious trap he was being forced into.

"No, Riley, we're not sending you alone." he raised his voice to a shout: "Sergeant!"

"Sir!" came the voice from the doorway. The Sergeant must have been standing just outside.

"Come in, Sergeant, come in. You are to proceed immediately to Dead Horse Marsh with special constable Riley and effect the capture of James Hatton."

"Yes, sir," said the sergeant stoically. "What force shall I take, sir?"

"No force, Sergeant, just yourself and Riley." He

leaned back and gave a little chuckle. "We can't afford to risk too many men on an expedition like this, Sergeant."

The sergeant said nothing. He stood unmoving, at attention. He must have been through this sort of thing before, thought Riley.

"Any question, Sergeant?"

"Yes, sir. Where is Dead Horse Marsh?"

"I'm having a little map prepared for you, Sergeant. It will be ready before you leave. Anything else?"

"No, sir."

"Then nothing remains except for me to wish you good fortune." The pig face was split with that travesty of a grin again. So might a pig in fact look if it tried to grin, thought Riley—a particularly ill-natured pig.

"May I speak, sir?" he said.

"Of course, Riley, of course."

"I would like to ask Miss Cabel a few questions if I may."

The grin slipped away, sideways, as though it was being pulled off, but then it came back again, hesitant, doubtful.

"All right, Riley, go ahead."

"Miss Cabel," said Riley, turning to Jane who raised her eyes and looked at him gently . . . but surely there was a spark of mirth somewhere in those attractive depths? "Miss Cabel, why exactly have you given this information about James Hatton."

"For the same reason I told you before," said Jane. "He killed my brother."

"But you remember the last time we had a conversation like this?"

"Of course I do." Strange how the Australian accent sounded almost pleasant on those treacherous, but lovely, lips.

"Then would you mind telling me where you were when I arrived at the shanty and found Hatton waiting for me?"

The little face became troubled. She hadn't had time to think that one out, Riley thought. She'd probably been hiding in the kitchen in fact. She brushed her hand across her nose and opened her mouth.

"I've already told you, Riley," said the sub-inspector heavily, "that I am completely satisfied with Miss Cabel's good faith. You may accept my word if you won't accept hers. It is not your place to make these investigations."

Riley sighed and turned to the sub-inspector.

"Yes, sir," he said.

"That will be all. Sergeant, see that you are both adequately equipped. Pick up that map and I'll expect to hear from you, or one of you, within a week."

Those blasted cicadas again, thought Riley, as he rode out of Goulburn with the Sergeant in the late afternoon. Riley was riding his police horse, complete with sword and carbine. He was dressed in one of Collingwood's white suits. He'd have to change before he went into the bush, he thought. The Sergeant, similarly mounted and armed, was wearing his operational uniform. They had their gear in rolls behind their saddles, having felt that pack horses would have slowed them down too much.

"Can you read that map?" said Riley.

"It doesn't matter," said the Sergeant, "I know where Dead Horse Marsh is anyway."

"Oh." Then after a while Riley said: "Did you read my last report about Jane Cabel?"

"No." said the Sergeant, "of course not."

"Well one of my recommendations was that she be charged with aiding and abetting James Hatton in attempting to murder me."

The Sergeant laughed.

"There's not a jury in the tablelands 'd bring in a verdict against Janey Cabel. Not in the whole Colony for that matter."

"Why not?"

"Gawd, you haven't been here long, have you?"

"No," said Riley.

"You can't put a woman before a jury, particularly not a pretty one. They never convict 'em."

"I see," said Riley.

A little later he said: "You realise this expedition is probably another trap, don't you?"

"Could be," said the Sergeant.

"Why do you suppose we're being sent on it?"

"Mad Mick hates your guts because you haven't been killed yet."

"So what are you doing here?"

"He hates mine too. He heard me call him Mad Mick once."

"I see."

And a little later: "You don't think it would be a good idea if we camped in the bush for a few days and then came back and reported no contact.'"

"No. Mad Mick'd find out. You can't do anything on the tablelands without everybody else knowing about it. Somebody'd be sure to spot us."

"So what do we do?"

"Ride out to Dead Horse Marsh, then ride back and report no contact."

"I see."

A few moments later the sergeant said explanatory:

"Mad Mick sends me out on a job like this every couple of months or so. I've got to obey orders. I'd get sacked if I didn't."

A hundred yards further on he said: "I've got a wife and three kids you see."

Riley said: "Of course it's just possible it may not be a trap. Hatton wouldn't have much interest in anybody but me, and he wouldn't know that Madden would send me after him."

"Oh yes he would," said the Sergeant, never taking his solemn eyes off the road ahead: "Anybody who knew Mad Mick would have bet a tenner on that."

"But does Hatton know—Mad Mick?"

"Everybody knows Mad Mick," said the Sergeant obscurely.

"Would you mind if we made a detour past Collingwood's station?" Riley said. "I could get hold of a decent horse and some guns. Probably get some for you too."

"We'll go round by the station if you like," said the Sergeant. "But I'll stick to what I've got. More than my job's worth to change horses, or use guns that aren't regulation."

More than your life's worth not to, thought Riley.

Once, as they jogged towards the station, he attempted a more general conversation with the Sergeant.

"Do you think they'll ever clear the bushrangers out?"

"Do a lot of troopers out of jobs if they ever do," said the Sergeant broodingly.

"Better just tell Collingwood we're going on a routine patrol," said Riley. "If he thought we were going any where near Hatton he'd want to come too. He's the enthusiastic type."

"All right," said the Sergeant.

It was a two day ride to the Dead Horse Marsh, right across the plateau of the tablelands, up over the hills that were the crests of mountains to the west, and imperceptibly down on a journey which would have eventually led to the great flat western plains. As they were making camp at sunset, on the day after they left Goulburn the sergeant said: "I wouldn't mind the reward that's out for Hatton. Five hundred quid each we'd get if we brought him in."

"Feeling tempted to try?" asked Riley.

"No," said the Sergeant firmly: "I'd just like the money."

"What would you do with it?" asked Riley.

"Go back to England," said the Sergeant promptly. Riley looked at the man's heavy sun-burned features in surprise. He'd thought Aldrych was an Australian.

"What part of England do you come from?"

"Liverpool".

"How long have you been out here?"

"Fifteen years."

Riley marvelled at the infectious qualities of the Australian accent. The man spoke as though he'd never been out of the colony in his life. Could there be anything in the theory that people's voices changed when they came here because they developed the habit of speaking with their mouths almost closed to keep out the summer heat and dust?

"I'd never have thought it," he said, studying his own mouth movements, and deciding that as far as he could make out, he was speaking with his mouth as open as usual. He wondered how he would sound after ten years in the colony. But surely to God he'd get out before that.

They kept the fire going after they'd eaten, not because it was cool. It was a hot and breathless night and they had to sit away from the flames. But a fire was strangely comforting in the loneliness of the bush.

"Do you suppose Hatton does have a *plant* in these marshes," Riley said in the quiet voice in which men speak to each other in the bush at night.

"He has a *plant* there all right," said the Sergeant. "We've known about it for months. But you can't get at it. It's right in the marshes. There's a track through, but no-one knows where it is . . . no trooper anyway. That's why they call it Dead Horse Marsh—because of the horses that have got bogged there and couldn't get out."

He poked at his teeth with a twig. "Quite a few cattle got lost there too," he added.

"What exactly do you suppose the sub-Mad Mick expects us to do?"

"Dunno," said the Sergeant, "don't think he cares. Just hopes we'll get shot."

"I suppose it's possible at that," said Riley.

"I won't," said the Sergeant confidently.

Riley lay long awake on his blanket that night, occasionally waving a small branch about his face in a futile attempt to discourage the mosquitoes. They hadn't bothered about tents on that hot, dry night and Riley gazed into the close stars, brilliant and so plentiful that they almost formed a solid canopy of white silver. If Hatton were really in the Dead Horse Marsh it would be very satisfying to kill him. He wanted Hatton to die, wanted him to die because Dave and Andy were dead, and for some strange and unfathomable reason he wanted him to die because John Cabel was dead. He wanted James Hatton to die and he wanted to kill him.

"Dermot Riley," he murmured, "you're a changed man, a changed man."

They'd left the road ten miles back and were winding single file along a cattle track.

They would come to another road shortly, the Sergeant had said, and, by sunset that day to a shanty quite near the Marsh. They would allow themselves to be seen at the shanty and that would be sufficient for word to get back to Goulburn that they'd been there. Then, the Sergeant had announced, they'd take off into the bush for a couple of days before beginning the journey back.

"Aren't we likely to run into trouble at the shanty?" Riley had asked.

"Not unless Hatton himself happens to be there. We'd better try and find out first whether he is or not. No-one else in his gang is likely to make trouble, no-one that I know of." He paused, then added: "I don't think so, anyway."

Riley was leading and had to keep Collingwood's hack reined in to prevent it leaving the Sergeant far behind. Riley also had one of Collingwood's breech-loading rifles in his saddle holder and three of Collingwood's revolvers in his belt. He'd brought his sword as well because he'd developed an affection for the weapon, as a man might for some sort of talisman, and there was no point in trying to hide his identity when he was travelling with a fully uniformed trooper. He'd even taken the trouble to put an edge on the blade.

The Sergeant was inclined to be talkative, maintaining a steady stream of conversation as the horses plodded along the path. Riley, in the lead, could hear him quite clearly, but to make himself heard he had to turn in the saddle. He found this wearing after an hour or so and restricted his replies to yes and no.

"Mind you," the Sergeant was saying, "you can be lucky in this business. I've known men with up to a thousand pounds or more on their heads brought in without firing a shot."

"Yes?" said Riley.

"They got Ben Hall over at Forbes that way only this year . . . last May it was."

"Mm," said Riley.

"You heard about Ben Hall, didn't you?" Riley had heard about Hall, the one time squatter whose first exploit on the road was to help Frank Gardiner hold up the gold coach at Eugowra Rock. Hall had assumed leadership of the gang when Gardiner had retired and gone to live peacefully in Queensland. Legends about Hall were still rife, and it appeared at one stage he had been as infamous on the tablelands as James Hatton, although he hadn't had his reputation for utterly callous brutality.

"Yes, I heard about him."

"Did you hear how they got him?"

"Not exactly."

"Well I'll tell you," said the sergeant accommodatingly. "He was playing about with this lubra ho was living with a half caste in a shack about twelve miles from Forbes."

"Mm," said Riley.

"Well the halfcaste didn't like this, naturally. Funny thing that. Coves like Hall get so sure of themselves that they think they can play around with another man's woman and expect the fella just to stand aside and bow politely.

"Well this half-caste didn't like it at all so one night, in May this was, old Ben's makin' hay in the shack and this halfcaste slips into town, into Forbes, and tells the troopers where Ben is. Can you hear me all right?"

"Yes, yes," said Riley, turning in the saddle. "Quite clearly. Go on."

"Well the boys there get all excited. No-one wants to tangle with Ben Hall, naturally, but then this is the first time anyone's got a good lead on him being anywhere by himself. He left his Mates Gilbert and Dunn behind when he went off after this lubra, which was only natural.

"Anyhow Jimmy Davidson—you run across Jimmy? No, you wouldn't have. He's a sub-inspector in the Lachlan Division; not a bad fellow, bloody sight better than Mad Mick anyway—he sets off into the bush with something like thirty men."

A huge frill necked lizard basking on a rock hissed its anger at Riley and his horse shied violently.

"Are those things dangerous?" said Riley, looking with aversion at the gaping jaws and yellow mouth. He was irresistibly reminded of the interior of sub-inspector Madden's mouth. Would Madden have a venomous bite? Probably.

"No," said the Sergeant, "not bad to eat if you ever run short of rations."

Better to starve, thought Riley. But then it probably wouldn't be really.

They resumed their peaceful journey along the downward sloping path. The Sergeant resumed his story, speaking a little louder now because the cicadas had started again.

Riley found he could hear the Sergeant quite clearly despite the pervading presence of the cicadas' rattle. He could hear the horses' hooves too. It was as though the cicadas created a sea of sound in which other sounds moved quite freely.

"Where was I? Ah yes. Anyhow it's obvious even to a bloody officer that Ben's gonna hear thirty men barging through the bush long before they get near him, so he calls out Billy Dargin. Now you wouldn't have heard about Billy. He's an abo. Old Freddie Pottinger put him on strength a couple of years' back. You heard of Freddie? He was a baronet our Freddie was. Funny fellow. Started off out here as a trooper and when they found he was a baronet they made him an inspector. Mightn't have been a bad trooper but he was a bloody awful officer, so they say. Anyway, I never met him myself. He shot himself in the end—they were gonna sack him because he couldn't catch Ben Hall, so he shot himself. Funny business."

Riley drowsed in the saddle, the cicadas and the Sergeant's monologue acting as a dual soporific.

"Anyhow, Billy Dargin was a tracker and a beaut he was too. Track goannas over an acre of rock, they say. Davidson sent Billy on to the shack to see if old Ben was still there."

Riley noticed that the Sergeant always spoke of Hall with a measure of affection.

"Another funny thing about that whole business," said the Sergeant who was so fond of digression that Riley was finding it difficult to follow the thread of his story," is that Billy once used to work for Ben. When Ben was a squatter Billy worked on his station. Old Freddie talked him into joining the force when he found out how he could track. They tell me it used to be as funny thing as you'd ever see to watch old Billy, wearing a rag of a coat, trying to line up on parade with the troopers and Freddie Pottinger having a fit every time he seen him.

"Anyhow, where was I?"

Riley didn't know.

"Ah yes, well, Billy goes on and creeps around the shack and finds there's no sign of Ben in the place. It's all dark and as far as he can make out the lubra's asleep inside by herself.

"Well I told you Billy was one miracle of a tracker, so damn me if he doesn't pick Ben's tracks up in the dark and follow him to his camp. Ben had camped only a mile or so away from the shack.

"Maybe he was tired out," the Sergeant gave a lubricous chuckle.

"Anyway Billy snoops around Ben, who's sleeping like the dead, but doesn't do anything about it. He hadn't been told to you see. He'd only been told to find Ben. Davidson had forgot to say anything about shooting him, and abo's aren't very bright. So old Billy slips back to the mob and tells them were Ben is.

"Jimmy Davidson gets all excited about this, so he gives Billy Dargin a revolver and tells him to go on up and shoot Ben. And the rest of the mob follows.

"Well no-one seems to know exactly what happened after that, but eventually it seems all these coves get up around Ben's camp, with Billy Dargin up front, and poor old Ben still sleepin' like the dead.

"It gets to be about dawn and these coves are still waiting around Ben's camp—why they didn't shoot him, or why Billy didn't shoot him I don't know. I suppose because they couldn't be sure it was Ben. It's hard to tell with a cove all wrapped up in a blanket on the ground. And it was May so I suppose he had his head wrapped up too.

"Anyhow eventually Ben wakes up and crawls out of his blankets and he's fully dressed with God knows how many revolvers in his belt.

"So someone shoots him. Gawd alone know who it was. Billy reckons it was him, but every other trooper in the mob said it was him.

"Old Ben staggers around for a bit, he was probably dead on his feet, but they reckoned he tried to pull out his revolvers. So Billy shoots him again — most of 'em agree it was Billy shot him second. So over Ben goes and the whole bloody mob rushes up and shoots him.

"You know he had thirty holes in him when they brought him into Forbes."

Riley had a vision of the triumphant procession moving into the township, the bushranger's shattered body hanging over a packhorse and the crowd lining the streets.

"Things quietened down a bit round here after they got Ben," said the Sergeant, " 'cause they got Gilbert and Dunn not long after. Then this fellow Hatton turned up and it all started over again.

"Funny thing that though, old Billy Dargin workin' for Ben and then ending up the cove that got him killed, even if he didn't kill him himself."

This reflection on the complexity of life seemed to provide the Sergeant with ample matter for contemplation, for he kept silent until they finally emerged onto the road, as he had predicted they would.

"Don't like this now," said the Sergeant. "If they're expecting us they might lay up for us between here and the shanty."

"Why not on the track?"

"No. That's only one of half a dozen ways onto this road."

"Well what do we do?" said Riley, looking down the length of dusty road, which began to dance in the distance in the shimmering heat.

"Could cut off into the bush," said the Sergeant, "get up onto the ridge. That'd take us almost to the shanty and we could have a good look at it before we went near it."

"Why not?"

"Hard going. Lot safer though."

"Then let's be safe by all means," said Riley, leading the way off the road into the scrub.

They had to lead the horses most of the way, weaving through trees and scrub, scrambling around outcrops of rock. Even on the top of the ridge the undergrowth was very dense. After two hours of it the horses' hides were streaked dark with sweat. Riley's own clothes were wet through, but the Sergeant, still in full uniform, seemed unperturbed.

About two miles along the crest of the ridge he paused.

"That's the marsh down there."

Riley looked down through a gap in the trees into a vast valley which seemed to cleave the slopes and run clear down through the foothills into the distant plains beyond. The bottom of the valley was very wide and flat. It was heavily overgrown with trees, but they were broken by many clear patches, patches of curiously vivid green.

"It looks easy enough to get through," Riley said.

"Don't you believe it. Most of the green you can see is water lily. Horse'd sink to its belly in it."

"And you really think Hatton has a *plant* in there?"

"I'm damn sure of it. He's been seen going in half a dozen times."

"How'd he find the path?"

"One of the locals told 'im I suppose. Plenty of people round here'd know the way in, or the ways in. There's probably half a dozen of 'em. But they'd never tell a trooper.

"Can't blame 'em," added the Sergeant tolerantly. "More 'n their life's worth if Hatton found out."

"No-one's ever tried to follow him in?" said Riley.

"What'd be the use? You couldn't take a troop in there. If you did they'd have to go slowly in single file one man could pick 'em off easily."

Riley looked thoughtfully down into the lush and treacherous valley, aware of an irrepressible spurt of excitement.

"The tracks are very narrow, are they?" he said.

"Well they must be," said the Sergeant. "Stands to reason. They aren't tracks exactly, they're just runs of solid ground, lot of it's under water. You go a foot or so either side and you'd sink."

"It's not quicksand is it? I mean a man could get out if he fell in?"

"A man could get out all right, but a horse couldn't. Not by itself."

"But a man would find it hard to walk through?"

"Bloody near impossible. He'd be swimming half the time, or wading through mud. Unless he found the track. The water lily 'd stop you too. You get all tangled up in that— you can't move through it."

"But listen," said Riley excitedly. "If there's anybody in there it must be possible to find some sort of tracks, at the edge of the marsh anyway; not the paths, just racks showing where horses went in?"

"I daresay," said the Sergeant suspiciously.

"And they'd be moving in an out. They wouldn't just stay ther ?"

"Yeah?" The Sergeant wa definitely on his guard now.

Riley stopped talking and looked down into the

valley, mocking himself for the rising excitement he could feel — aware of an idea welling within him which he knew he would have to follow to completion, and, somewhere more remotely knowing a half ashamed twinge of lust for the smell of burned powder fired in anger.

"You realise," he said flatly, "that two men—under cover in the swamp—could slaughter any number of men trying to get through it."

"Here don't be bloody silly," said the Sergeant in alarm, "I thought you were a sensible sort of cove."

Riley smiled. He'd thought that about himself, once.

"Let's go down and have a look around," he said.

"What. Round the marsh?" The sergeant's voice had risen sharply.

Riley nodded.

"Don't be bloody silly," said the Sergeant, almost imploringly now.

"Look," said Riley, with an earnestness he didn't feel. "You look at it. It's just a chance, but supposing you found where they went in. I guarantee you could trace that track for half a mile or so, even if you had to wade all the way to do it—but you say it's not quicksand so why not? All right, so you trace out a section of the path—you set up at one point and I set up at another a hundred yards away, along the track. We could have perfect cover—up a tree even if you like. We wait until they get between us and we've got 'em. They can't move fast, they can't get past us. They can't go off the track. We wouldn't even have a fight—they'd have to surrender."

The Sergeant was looking at him as though he had suddenly gone insane. Perhaps he had.

"But how long are you gonna wait in the bloody marsh?" he almost howled.

"Just a few days," said Riley cajolingly. He couldn't rid his mind of a vision of James Hatton riding slowly through the marsh, picking his way, with Riley's rifle sights lined up on his great shaggy head—"Just a few days. We could make ourselves perfectly comfortable."

That was going a bit far, he thought, but it needn't be all that bad. They could set up a watching system, taking it in turns to guard the approaches.

"Have you ever camped in a marsh," said the Sergeant.

"No," said Riley, in fairness. "No, I haven't."

"The bloody mosquitoes 'd kill you. They'd carry you away, you and your bloody horse and your gear as well," said the Sergeant, moved to eloquence by his consternation. "And what are you going to do if they come through at night?"

"They wouldn't come through at night," said Riley, "no-one would try to move through that sort of country in the dark.

But the Sergeant was not disposed to reasonable argument.

"No," he said, "Come on. Let's go and poke our noses into that shanty. That's bloody dangerous enough without mucking about in bloody marshes." He started off along the ridge "I thought you were a sensible sort of cove," he added aggrievedly.

"There's a lot of reward money involved," said Riley.

"You're not dead long enough to spend it," said the Sergeant obscurely, and while Riley was trying to fathom that out he saw a long, thin stream of smoke reaching up into the sky from the depth of the marshes.

"Look at that," he said.

"Bloody remarkable," said the Sergeant bitterly,

"bloody remarkable." He stopped hauling at his horse's head.

"Look son," he said heavily. "I don't know what you think, but I don't think Janey Cabel's a nice reliable sort of girl. If she put Mad Mick up to sending someone out here it's because bloody Hatton wanted her to and he's waiting for that silly bloody someone to shove his silly bloody head into a noose. And I mean a noose."

"I couldn't agree with you more. It's a trap, an obvious trap. But don't you see, there's no trap in that marsh. That's the last place he'd expect to find anybody."

"And it's the last bloody place he'll find me," said the Sergeant, starting off again.

Riley watched him go, aware that the Sergeant's was the more sane attitude—that there was very little impulse for a near middle-aged man with three children to come on this slightly absurd venture. In fact he couldn't understand why there was any impulse for him to go himself, but there was, an irresistible impulse.

"Well listen," he called, "I'm going down. I'll meet you somewhere in a couple of days. Where abouts?"

The Sergeant stopped. Turned. Looked heavily at Riley then down at the marsh. Slowly he brought his horse's head round and came back to Riley.

"All right," he said, unemotionally. "You stupid, stupid bastard."

It wasn't until an hour later when they were almost at the bottom of the slope running into the valley, that Riley realised the Sergeant had probably changed his mind because he was afraid Riley would report his failure to co-operate.

Riley almost said something about it, but didn't. What was there to say? The Sergeant was morosely silent.

The tracks into the marsh were easy enough to find. The hoof marks of half a dozen horses were plain in the boggy ground at the bottom of the slope. About twenty yards further in was a disturbed area where it seemed a horse might have floundered off the hidden path.

"That smoke's about two miles in there," said Riley. "What's the nearest way to the road from here?"

"Straight back behind us," said the Sergeant.

"Then it's probable that they've come off the road, gone in here and made their way through to where that fire is."

The Sergeant grunted.

"If we can get in there about half a mile we'd be right," Riley said. "What we want is two patches of scrub with about a hundred yards or so of clear marsh in between."

The Sergeant grunted again.

Riley looked at the mass of water lilies stretching out to the first clump of trees. They were so thick it seemed possible to walk on them, an almost continuous carpet of wide flat pads.

The Sergeant spoke voluntarily for the first time in half an hour. "Well if we're going in let's go in; but for God's sake don't hang round here in the open."

"Look," said Riley. "I don't mind if you don't come, I can probably manage this quite well alone." He couldn't. It needed two men. Otherwise the bushrangers could simply turn round and go the other way when they were ambushed, and leave him stranded, where he was, forever if necessary.

"I'll come," said the Sergeant.

Not enthusiastic, but willing thought Riley. Which was all right. All the trooper had to do was shoot. Riley wished he'd been able to persuade him to borrow one of Collingwood's carbines. Pity the enthusiastic Swede wasn't here. He would have enjoyed this.

"I suppose I'd better wade in," Riley said speculatively

"As you like," said the Sergeant.

Riley eyed the water lilies doubtfully. He had suddenly remembered the prevalence of snakes in the district. The marshes were probably crawling with them. He saw himself splashing about in the mud, unable to move quickly, face to face with some hissing venomous serpent.

"I don't see why we shouldn't take the horses in," he said. "It's easy enough to follow these tracks."

"You get a horse stuck in there and you've lost him," said the Sergeant.

"But if the others didn't get stuck we won't. We can go exactly the same way as they went."

The Sergeant said nothing, but his expression was pained. Riley felt he was being specious himself. He had, after all, spoken somewhat grandly of wading in and making sure of the path. But it was perfectly true that it would be quite simple to follow the tracks of the horses that had already been through; the smashed and broken lilies and the mud that hung in the still water were an infallible guide.

"I'll go in and try," said Riley, "you wait here."

"No," said the Sergeant, "I'll come."

"There's no need to," said Riley.

"I'm not going to bloody well hang around here by myself," said the Sergeant bitterly. "Did it ever strike you, you bloody hero, that more of these bastards might come in through here at any minute, or that some of them might come out."

It had occurred to Riley, but that was just part of the calculated risk. There had been nothing he could do about it, so he had put it out of his mind. He was uncomfortably reminded of another calculated risk he had taken when he had tried to blow up the cave on Lightning Fork Ridge.

"Alright, come on," he said. And he urged his horse down from the firm ground into the edge of the marsh.

"There's only about an hour of daylight left," said the Sergeant.

"That should give us enough time to find a place. We'll camp the night and see if anybody comes through tomorrow."

"Bloody wonderful," said the Sergeant.

The horses sank to their hocks, but the ground beneath the water seemed quite firm. Riley let his horse take its own time, guiding it gently along the path of broken lilies which appeared to be leading directly to a grove of trees some distance away. The Sergeant followed very closely behind him, Riley heard him mutter occasionally, but he didn't say anything aloud.

Riley suddenly realised that the rhythmic throb of sound that filled the air was no longer coming from the cicadas; it was from frogs. He could see them leaping among the lilies, disturbed by the horses hooves, yellowish brown frogs with white underbellies, small ones only an inch or two long, millions of frogs.

The noise was more penetrating than the cicadas and Riley found he could hardly hear the horses' hooves splashing in the water. Which meant he wouldn't be able to hear anybody approaching from the other side of the grove of trees to which they were heading. That too, he told himself, was part of the calculated risk; but the calculations were becoming a little too wild.

A group of large, long legged white birds were feeding in the marsh not far to Riley's left. They had long fine bills and appeared to be searching for some delicacy. Probably frogs, he thought. They didn't even raise their heads as the horses plodded by.

There was one major flaw in his plan, Riley thought. Even if they managed to cut off one party of bushrangers in a stretch of swamp, there probably would be more at the camp. But they would take a long time to get through the swamp, even if, as seemed extremely improbable, they heard the sound of shots over the croaking of the frogs. There was a certain amount of chance in every action of this type, he reasoned, and all that was to be hoped was that Hatton was in any party they did happen to cut off. Riley saw himself riding into Goulburn with Hatton's body hung over a horse. Would Hatton have more than thirty holes in him, as Ben Hall had had? Riley didn't mind if he did.

They found the clump of trees was growing on almost dry ground. It was soft and they could see the tracks of the horses, but the party had split up and the hoofmarks were spread erratically through the trees. They looked very fresh. Riley stopped and tried to listen, but there was only the sound of the frogs. He turned and looked at the Sergeant, but the Sergeant had turned also and was looking back the way they had come. He apparently didn't see anything and he turned around. He caught Riley's eye and looked away quickly.

Riley hoped they would find the sort of territory he was looking for soon. He didn't want to penetrate too far into the swamp and he didn't want to get too near the bushrangers' camp. And he didn't want to try the Sergeant's thin drawn co-operation much further either. Of course, he reflected, there was no reason why the particular relationship of scrub and water he wanted should exist in the marsh at all.

But it did. He found it as they emerged on the other side of the grove of trees.

The water lilies stretched out for about two hundred yards, and there ahead was another thick clump of trees. Riley could see the trail of the horses through the lilies leading directly to the trees. That apparently was the pattern of the paths through the marsh — a series of islands joined by strips of more or less firm ground below water level. There were a lot of reeds here and Riley guessed they were growing in treacherous ground. He saw how the trail they were following weaved carefully away from them. He wondered why the paths through the marsh had remained such a secret. It was perfectly simple to follow them. Or perhaps it was only possible for a stranger if he followed closely on the tracks of whoever had gone in first. Perhaps more simply, nobody had wanted to try to find the way in.

He went over to the Sergeant.

"This'll do," he said. "You stay here. Make a camp over to one side in the trees. I'll go across to those trees over there."

The Sergeant grunted.

"There's not much point in signalling each other. We'll see what we're after. If they come through, we'll wait until they reach the middle and I'll call on 'em to surrender. They won't, of course, and then we'll start shooting."

"And how long are we supposed to wait around for this to happen?" the Sergeant said heavily.

"Well, through tomorrow at any rate," said Riley.

"I'll come back tomorrow evening and we'll have a talk about it."

"Yeah," said the Sergeant. "We'll have a talk about it."

"You'd better have one of these revolvers," said Riley. "And some cartridges."

"Yeah, alright."

It would have been much more to the point if he'd sunken his prejudices and taken the rifle and revolvers that were offered him at Collingwood's station, thought Riley, but then he hadn't expected to be involved in a situation like this.

"We'd better not light fires."

"Thanks," said the Sergeant. "Thanks for that bit of advice."

There would be no reconciliation between them, Riley realised, until they left this marsh, probably not even then. He had forfeited the Sergeant's respect. He wasn't sure that he hadn't forfeited his own. Why was he doing this anyway?

"I'll see you tomorrow then," he said shortly, and sent his horse forward into the marsh. He had no doubts about the Sergeant. He would stay in the trees and he would shoot when required. He was much too anxious about his job not to do that. Riley felt a sense of guilt in having used such a lever to force the man to come with him. Not that he'd done it deliberately, but the effect was much the same as far as the Sergeant was concerned. A remarkably effective lever it was too, although that was not beyond understanding in a colony where an out of work trooper would not be exactly likely to find employment promptly.

Riley felt very alone and exposed as he moved out into the marsh. The sun was dropping low and the reeds cast long shadows over the water lilies. The marsh seemed to be in a constant turmoil of small movement as the frogs leaped and swam in a widening pool around the horse. Now and then there were some deeper swirling movements and Riley thought of snakes. But it could have been eels, or even fish. Once he saw a strange creature on a tuft of grass rising out of the water. It seemed to consist of a slightly rounded shell from which four scrawny legs protruded. From the front, static and reptilian, emerged a long grey neck and a head of ancient, unemotional evil. Riley tried to move his horse away from it, but did not dare diverge from the defined path of disturbed lily. The horse took no notice of the creature which did not move, apart from sharply drawing in its head, then poking it out again cautiously.

About half way between the clumps of trees Riley rode up onto a wide patch of soggy, moss grown ground. It was another of the islands in the marsh except that it had no trees on it. About fifty yards in width, it was roughly where he would want the bush-rangers to be when he opened fire on them, except that he didn't want them to be able to move around. Not that it would do them much good. They could dismount here and fire from behind their horses, but it would be only a matter of time before a man hidden in the trees picked them off. If they tried to ride off through the marsh they would be finished. A horse could never go at more than a walk through the lilies. It was a magnificent plan, Riley thought with satisfaction, if it ever reached that stage. And it could, it well could.

He rode off the high land into the water. About seventy yards now to the trees. He should have suggested the Sergeant keep his horse well out of the way. It might neigh if it heard other horses approaching. But then the Sergeant hadn't been exactly receptive of advice. Anyway he'd almost certainly think of it himself. And then it didn't matter, come to that, because nothing could be heard over the din of the frogs. He wondered whether they had periods of silence like the cicadas. He wondered whether there was such a thing as a prolonged silence in the colony. Probably not. That was probably why all the colonials were half insane. That was probably what was wrong with him. He'd been driven off his head by incessant noise.

Riley turned and looked back to the trees he'd left behind and saw with an awful sense of wrongness in the scheme of things that the Sergeant was riding at full gallop across the marsh towards him.

The Sergeant was riding at full gallop across the marsh. Riley stared. It wasn't possible. But it was happening. And it was happening silently. The frogs drowned all noise of that wild ride. Riley could only see the violent splashes at the horse's hooves. The Sergeant was looking over his shoulder. Somebody was following him. Somebody had startled him out of the cover of the trees. And he was trying to gallop across the marsh to Riley.

Riley watched, suspended in fascination. The horse had to fall. It had to fall or flounder into the marsh off the path. No horse could gallop over that spongy surface for any distance. The Sergeant was aiming the revolver behind him. Perhaps he was firing, Riley couldn't hear. Why didn't the fool get off the horse and try to run? He was likely to kill himself when the horse fell.

The horse fell. Silently and predictably it went over over on its shoulders. The Sergeant came off heavily, over the head, on his back in the water. Still Riley could hear nothing. The lack of sound took the reality from the scene. It was like watching a series of paintings; fluid tableaux of action. The horse, with a great flurry of water, scrambled to its feet and plunged out into the marsh. It went five yards then sank down to its belly and stayed there. It was as though somehow it had suddenly been driven into the ground.

The Sergeant was on his feet again. He was pointing his revolver back into the trees. Then the trooper turned and came blundering across the water lilies towards Riley.

Riley saw a man riding out of the trees, walking his horse carefully along the path, a revolver raised in one hand.

It was James Hatton. No-one else was that big. No-one else had that beard.

You poor. bloody fool, Riley, he thought bitterly, you poor, bloody fool of a would-be hero. You've killed that trooper as surely as if you shot him through the head yourself. You blundering fool.

Riley saw the Sergeant, inevitably he felt, stagger and quite slowly, fall to his knees. Then he lay down. But he wasn't dead. He was holding himself up on one elbow. Keeping his head clear of the water.

Riley, wondering why in the name of Heaven he hadn't done it before, urged his horse back through the marsh. There was no point in trying to gallop. No pointing even in dismounting and trying to wade. There was no way he could reach the trooper before Hatton.

The Sergeant was crawling now, crawling towards his horse. He'd drown if he went off the path. What the hell was he after?

Hatton was still shooting at him. Why didn't the Sergeant shoot back? He'd probably lost his revolver when he fell. That was why he was crawling to his horse. He was after his carbine.

Cursing himself Riley remembered the rifle in his own saddle holster. He yanked it out and tried to line the sights on Hatton. He couldn't do it. Not sitting on a moving horse. He fired anyway.

Then he slipped off the horse and knelt in the water. It was clammy around his thighs. The water on his skin made him feel strangely vulnerable to snakes. His hands were shaking. Why the hell were his hands shaking? He fired.

Hatton was off his horse. He'd shot him. He'd killed James Hatton. No he hadn't. Damn and blast it. The man had dismounted and was walking forward behind his horse. Then shoot the horse.

Fumbling badly Riley reloaded. The Sergeant had reached his own horse. But he wasn't doing anything. He was just lying across the saddle.

Riley lined his sights on Hatton's horse. Found the animal's chest in the V then brought up the foresight. Just have the top of the foresight in the bottom of the V. Squeeze the trigger, squeeze it slowly.

He fired. He missed. Then the rifle exploded in his hands. But it couldn't have. It wasn't even loaded. It had reared up and torn itself away from him. His hands were numb, shocked. Then he understood. A bullet had hit the rifle. Hatton had fired at him with a revolver and hit him for all practical purposes at more than eighty yards!

Don't stand there like a bloody fool. Where was the rifle? God it was gone. Sunk in the water lilies. But not far. He could find it. But he didn't have the time. He didn't have time to grope around in the mud while Hatton was advancing on the trooper. But the trooper was as good as dead. There was nothing he could do for him. All he could do was kill Hatton. But he couldn't even do that if he floundered around on his hands and knees in the mud.

Riley threw himself back in the saddle. He forced the horse into a trot. It might fall but at least he was moving at a speed that would make it hard for Hatton to hit him. He had his two revolvers in his belt. But he didn't even bother pulling them out. He could never hit anything with them. Not at this range. Not moving.

Hatton was almost on top of the trooper now. He came out from behind his horse. He must have realised Riley wasn't shooting at him. He raised his revolver. He was going to shoot the Sergeant. Shoot him as he lay helpless across his bogged horse. No he wasn't. He'd put the pistol back in his belt. He leaned forward, stretching out towards the horse. He was taking something from it. The carbine. Well that would take him time. He was looking at it. Then he flung it away. Now he was after something else at the saddle. He stood up. A flash of silver ran from his hand. He'd taken the trooper's sword.

Riley pulled out a pistol and fired as he saw Hatton raise the sword. But the shot didn't even make the bushranger falter as he brought the sword down in a long, sweeping blow at the Sergeant. And he did it again. The Sergeant fell forward across the horse.

"You bloody swine," sobbed Riley, "you bloody swine." But he didn't know whether he meant himself or Hatton.

Hatton was back on his horse, riding towards Riley, riding at a trot. His revolver was in his hand, raised. Riley heard a bullet rushing past his head. It must have been very close. He wouldn't have heard it otherwise. Hatton was alone. That was one good thing. Although he might have more men back in the trees. No. He wouldn't have. They would have come out after him by now. Or they would have started shooting. Another bullet went past him. He might as well shoot. He might be lucky. But it would be better to keep his revolvers loaded until they closed. But just one shot. Just one shot, like a man buying just one card in a card game. He pulled out a revolver and fired, not bothering to try to aim. Nothing happened. Better not fire again. Not at this range. Hatton had stopped. He was sitting on his horse doing something with his hands. He was reloading his revolver. Try a shot at him now? Get off the horse and try a shot? Not with the revolver. God if only he had the rifle still. But then Hatton wouldn't have stopped if he'd had the rifle. Try another shot? No use. Keep the revolvers loaded. How many cartridges did he have in the chambers? Five in one and three in the other. Hatton would have ten. He was sure to have two revolvers. Possibly more.

Riley reined the horse in. Better reload. No point in hurrying now. The Sergeant was dead. All that was going to happen was that he and Hatton were going to meet and fight in the marsh. It didn't matter where in the marsh. He reloaded quickly and resumed the steady trot towards Hatton.

Another bullet passed him. That meant he had ten shots and Hatton had nine, probably. He must count the bullets. In a quick rush at the end extra bullets in the chambers of a revolver could mean victory. But Hatton would realise that. Riley was dimly aware of a sense of satisfaction that there was no alternative to his moving in to fight with Hatton. He wanted to anyway, but he couldn't do anything else. Flight the other way would only mean eventually running into the bushrangers' camp. He couldn't move in any other direction than along the track of trampled water lilies. He had to go to Hatton. And one of them would die.

One of them must die. He had known it would come to this; he didn't know how he had known, but he had. He hadn't known it would be here, in this green wet world of croaking frogs.

God but he was sorry about the trooper. Dead on the water lilies, never again to see the wife and three children in Goulburn.

Hatton had stopped firing now. He was probably waiting for the range to close to certainty. Riley quite clearly saw his own body lying face downwards in the water lilies. Don't think of that. Don't think of anything. Just ride forward and then shoot and pray to God Almighty that you're luckier than you deserve.

Riley felt a change in his horse's gait and looked down to see that he was riding over moss. The island between the clumps of trees. Hatton must be nearly at the other side of it. He was. Only fifty yards away now.

Riley kicked his heels into horse's ribs and sent it charging forward at a gallop. His main hope—his only hope—lay in getting in close and relying on chance rather than skill. Move in close and shoot fast. He lay down low over the horse's neck, his revolver held out level with the animal's head. It didn't matter if it shied when he fired. The more it moved about the better. He heard a bullet thud into the horse's flesh, but it didn't seem to hurt it. He was forty yards away now. Thirty. Twenty. Hatton had ridden onto the firmer ground, had reined in and was waiting for him. Aiming carefully from his horse. Ten yards. His horse's hooves were thudding wetly on the moss. Strange. He could hear them clearly. He fired and kept on firing, fired five times while his horse galloped over ten yards. And he missed every time.

He wheeled round as the water lilies swept in towards

him. Hatton was still in the one place, his revolver held out in a straight and level arm. Riley thrust his empty revolver back into his belt and pulled out the other one. He was almost on Hatton now. Cannon into him. Knock him down. He dragged his horse's head over, but Hatton spurred to one side and Riley galloped past, getting off two shots almost in the bushranger's face. Hatton had fired at him too. He didn't know how many times. He thought he'd felt the powder burn his face. But he couldn't have. He hadn't been that close. He was at the other end of the island now. And Hatton was still in the same place, reloading.

How many cartridges were in his own revolver? He didn't know. Charge down now and try to get Hatton while he was reloading. No. His own revolvers might be empty.

He reined in and began to reload. Immediately Hatton raised his revolver and fired. The bullet chopped a neat hole in Riley's horse's right ear. The horse reared wildly. Riley brought it down and then he saw that Hatton was galloping at him. Riley raised his revolver, aimed it over his horse's head and pulled the trigger. The hammer clicked home on an empty chamber. But he had cartridges in that revolver. At least two. Damn it! He'd moved them round when he began to reload.

He sent the horse into a gallop, straight at Hatton. His best chance was to keep moving. Even Hatton riding a galloping horse couldn't hope to hit a man on a galloping horse. Riley went down over his horse's neck again and began pulling the trigger of his revolver. It clicked on an empty chamber once more then fired two shots.

Hatton went past in a blur but Riley saw the flash

of white teeth in the mass of beard. The man was grinning, or snarling.

Hatton must have fired at him, but he'd heard nothing, no rush of bullets, no sound of firing, nothing. The frogs had started again. Had they ever stopped?

Riley reined in. Hatton had stopped about forty yards away and was reloading. Was this another trap? It didn't matter if it was. He had to reload now anyway.

Riley was pleased to find his movements were deft and calm as he slipped the cartridges into the chambers. His hands had stopped trembling now. There was blood running down his horse's shoulder. God help him if his horse was killed, or went lame.

A bullet thudded into his saddle and his horse shied nervously.

Riley kept a short rein but tickled his horse's ribs with his heels, making it dance spasmodically. Hatton was aiming carefully, sitting still on his horse. Let him shoot. His chances of hitting a moving target weren't high. Let him shoot and count the bullets. That was two. Ride in towards him, gallop, now turn and go back. Three bullets. Four. God but the man was good. Eventually a bullet would hit him. How many had hit the horse now? Hatton fired again. Five bullets. That meant he had only one loaded revolver. Probably.

Riley wheeled round and charged at Hatton again, firing as he went. Hatton was firing back at him, emptying his second revolver. The hammer of Riley's revolver was hitting empty chambers. He tried to thrust it back into his belt, cursed when it slipped and fell to the ground, clawed out his second revolver and fired, once, twice. Keep some bullets, keep some and hope to sweet God that Hatton runs out. Hatton was moving now. Galloping towards him. He wouldn't do that if he had cartridges left. Riley reined in, so suddenly his horse went back on its haunches. He held his revolver out, waiting for the barrel to fall level with Hatton. It took so long, so long for a rearing horse's hooves to reach the ground. But there was Hatton, feet away, moving, but surely to God he couldn't miss. Quickly he pulled the trigger, again and again, almost weeping at the time it took just to pull his finger back a quarter of an inch, feeling the throb of the weapon in his hand as he fired, pouring the bullets at the rushing mass of horse and man sweeping past him.

He was at the edge of the water lilies again. Hatton had halted and was reloading. He still hadn't hit the bloody man. They looked across at each other, tacitly observing a minor truce.

This was the way it was going to be, thought Riley, a series of charges across the island, firing at each other until finally one bullet struck home. And he only had one revolver now. Better make his charge before Hatton had time to load both of his.

Riley kicked at his horse, and went careering towards Hatton again, terribly aware that the odds were heavily against him. Hatton was much more skilful than he, and now he was twice as well armed. He was waiting there, sitting on his horse, levelling his revolver. Riley drummed his heels into the horses ribs, faster, you bloody animal, faster. This time he heard the whistling crack of a bullet cleave past his ear. Damn it to dear Heaven one had to hit him soon. He had his own pistol levelled, but didn't fire. He seesawed the reins, forcing the horse to swerve violently from side to side. Careful you'll pull it over on its neck. Damn it, this was suicide. there must be another way.

There was.

He thought of it and started to do it in the one

moment, as his horse carried him down upon Hatton. He switched his revolver to his left hand and began shooting, letting go of the reins. He still hadn't reached Hatton. Everything seemed to be happening so slowly, with such awful clarity.

He snatched his sword from its scabbard, gave it one half whirl around his head and lashed at Hatton. He felt the sword bit at something and then he was past. He wheeled. Hatton was riding away from him. His revolver must be empty. Had he hurt him?

Riley fired once after the retreating bushranger, then his revolver was empty.

Something was wrong about Hatton. His movements were strange. He stopped his horse now and was fumbling with something. He must be reloading, but there was something peculiar about him.

Riley's own revolver was reloaded now, and he began to walk the horse across the island, keeping his sword in his right hand, the revolver in his left with the reins.

.He saw a revolver on the ground. He could use that. It wasn't his own. It must be Hatton's. He must have knocked it from his hand with the sword. But he daren't get off the horse to get it. It would take too long. But Hatton still had his back to him. What the hell was happening?

Then he saw a human thumb and a finger, obscenely detached from a hand, lying on the damp ground.

Riley reined in his horse and stared in disbelief at the grisly morsels of flesh. So that was what was wrong with Hatton. Riley had chopped half his hand off.

He looked across at Hatton again. The man was facing him now, waiting, a revolver held in his right hand. He was cradling his left hand on the saddle.

With a hand shattered like that Hatton would not possibly be able to load a revolver. If that revolver he had in his hand was empty, or when he had fired the cartridges that were in it, he would be finished.

Riley raised his revolver and fired a shot, not even bothering to try to aim, simply trying to tempt Hatton into firing. The bushranger sat motionless on his horse. Riley slipped another cartridge into the empty chamber.

He was feeling strangely cautious now. The knowledge that Hatton must soon be helpless made him nervous of last minute, accidental defeat.

He thought of calling on Hatton to surrender, but abandoned the idea as foolish. Why should the man surrender? He'd only be hanged. His best chance lay in keeping the game going until some of his gang showed up. And Riley's best chance was in finishing it quickly for the same reason.

He gave a yell to bolster his own courage as much as anything and urged his horse into a gallop. Hatton immediately began to gallop towards him. His revolver was empty. He wouldn't have moved otherwise. Riley fired his revolver quickly, then raised his sword. He saw Hatton wrench his horse's head and veer away to the left. Riley galloped past, his sword swinging harmless in the air.

But now, he thought, with elation, it was just a matter of time. He would reload and quietly stalk the bushranger, stalk him to his death.

He swung round and saw that Hatton had dismounted on the other side of the island. He picked something off the ground and leaped back into the saddle.

The other revolver. Riley cursed himself for his idiocy, but it wasn't; Hatton had a sword in his hand. The trooper's sword. He must have carried it with him and then dropped it when Riley first charged him.

And now Hatton was charging, galloping furiously across the island with the sword above his head.

Riley fumbled with the cartridges. It was awkward with the sword in his hand, but he had to keep it there. He had two in the chambers. No time for more. He raised the revolver. He shouldn't fire yet. But he didn't know whether there was a cartridge or empty chamber in the breech. He pulled the trigger. Empty. Again. It fired. He had one more shot and Hatton was almost on him. He fired, then ducked and swung his horse to one side. He heard the bushranger shouting and heard the sword whistle through the air. Viciously he pulled his horse's head round. Hatton had turned too. He was only feet away. Moving in with the sword swinging.

Riley still had his sword in his left hand. He raised it above his head and caught Hatton's blade as it came down. The steel rang loud and Riley felt his arm tingle as the shock went through the guard.

Hatton pulled his sword back and swung it around at Riley's chest. Riley dropped his arm and caught the blade on his guard. He tried to thrust the point at Hatton's throat but Hatton bore down on his own blade and the two men sat their horses, leaning their weight against their swords, glaring into each other's faces. Hatton's teeth were still bared. He was snarling. Riley glimpsed the mangled left hand. Hatton had wrapped his reins around his wrist.

Simultaneously both men pulled away. Riley slipped his sword into his right hand. He wanted to load his revolver, but Hatton would never give him time for that.

Hatton levelled his sword like a lance and came charging at Riley.

It was all happening so slowly, Riley thought, and knocked Hatton's blade aside with his own sword. It was all happening so slowly, but his own movements were slow, too. If only his body would work as fast as his brain.

Hatton's horse cannoned into his and Hatton struck at his head with the hilt of the sword. Riley ducked and tried to stab Hatton in the chest, but there wasn't room. He couldn't pull his sword back far enough.

The two horses broke away and Hatton gave a back-handed swipe which missed.

Riley waited, his sword thrust out level with his shoulder. Hatton moved his horse in, warily, his sword held above his head. He swiped downwards at Riley's blade and Riley moved it to one side, swung it round over his horse's head and cracked Hatton across the neck with the blunt edge. The bushranger grunted and moved back. Riley cursed the fact that he'd hit him with the blunt edge. He'd have taken half his head off if he had hit him with the sharpened blade. But the blow should have knocked him off his horse. The man wasn't even stunned. He was like a bull.

But this was the moment to take the fight to him if ever there was one.

Riley urged his horse over, holding his sword back-handed above his horse's head so that he could swipe with the sharp edge of the blade.

Hatton struck out at Riley's horse, trying to stab it in the eyes. Riley knocked his sword down, then moved past him, lashing out at the back of the man's neck as he went.

Something brilliantly hot hit him across the bridge of the nose.

Blinded, he kicked his horse into a gallop. Hatton's sword had caught him across the face. He couldn't see. Where the hell did the marsh begin? He pulled on the reins, and swung around. His eyes began to clear. Hatton was coming at him.

Riley thrust his sword forward and made his horse charge towards Hatton. But it was no use. He couldn't see. The horses collided. Something unbearably hard hit him across the head. Hatton's face was almost in his. He actually felt the man's breath. What was happening? The horses were going down. They were falling. There was Hatton below him, falling towards the ground. But Riley's mind was leaving him. Even as he fell he was slipping away into blackness. Was this death? He could see Hatton's throat, white under his beard. The man seemed to be upside down. Riley was taking a long time to fall. He tried to stab at Hatton's throat.

Then there was just black, unendurable blackness, swamping him and then nothing.

He became conscious quickly, without confusion. There was no fear. If he was not dead something must have happened. What had happened? He sat up.

The two horses were standing side by side a few yards away.

Hatton lay beside him, Riley's sword clean through his throat.

Riley stood up tentatively. He felt nothing, no elation, no satisfaction. Hatton was dead. But it was more of an accident than anything else.

Riley felt his nose and his head. There were large lumps, but no cuts. He wasn't badly hurt.

He looked at Hatton. The man's eyes were open, and his white teeth were still showing. He looked handsome and generous in death. The sword looked improbable thrust through his throat and into the soft ground beneath him. With his arms outspread he looked like some magnificent specimen of insect pinned to a board.

Riley tried to work out what happened. He remembered trying to stab Hatton as they fell. But that had been a feeble business. He must have just caught him with the point and then thrust it on through by the dead weight of his own unconscious, falling body.

This corpse was worth one thousand pounds. The thought was shocking, and yet unbearably attractive. One thousand pounds clear could mean an end to this barbaric colony . . . an end to the sub-inspector and an end to his own inexplicable temptations towards violence. How did he know it was one thousand pounds? The Sergeant had told him. God in Heaven, the Sergeant, the poor dead instrument of Riley's actions.

He looked across the marsh. The Sergeant was sitting in the saddle of his bogged horse, waving at Riley.

"Course I wasn't bloody well dead," said the Sergeant, when Riley had got him across to the island and was trying to clean mud from two deep cuts across the back of his neck and shoulders, "Course I wasn't dead, but I wasn't going to let Hatton know that."

"But you were shot," said Riley. "Where did he get you?"

"In the bloody backside. Dropped me like an ox."

"Well for God's sake let me clean it up."

"Be damned. Let's get out of here before any more of his mob turns up."

"But are you alright?"

"Course I'm not bloody well all right, but I'll be a damn sight worse if we stay here."

Queasily Riley pulled his sword from Hatton's throat and wiped it on the moss. He led Hatton's horse over and hoisted the heavy limp body on to it It took him a long time.

"Cut the bloody head off," the Sergeant said, "That's all we want." But that was too macabre for Riley.

He wondered foolishly about the finger and thumb lying on the moss. He didn't like leaving part of a human body abandoned like that. But there was nothing else he could do. He thought of throwing it out into the marsh, but he couldn't bring himself to touch it.

There was no hope of hauling the Sergeant's horse out of the marsh. Riley shot it. Then he helped the Sergeant onto his own horse and, taking the reins of Hatton's horse led the way out of the swamp. He hated wading in the tangled water-lilies; but he didn't see any snakes.

They made their way back to Goulburn along the route they had come, but they were slower now because Riley had to walk all the way.

Each night he did his best to dress the Sergeant's wounds, but they were beginning to fester. They had a lot of trouble with Hatton's body. Riley had to get it off the horse each night and on again in the mornings.

He insisted on leaving it, wrapped in a blanket, some distance from their camp each night.

"Be careful with that bloody thing," the Sergeant grumbled. "It's worth a thousand pounds to us."

Riley rode back into Goulburn two weeks later for the inquest. He was still happy, still singing. He rode into the barracks and met the Sergeant, hobbling with a walking stick, but looking even glummer than that warranted.

"Haven't you heard?"

"Heard what?" said Riley.

"About the reward."

"What about the reward?" Riley felt a deep, hollow fear.

"We don't get it."

"What do you mean we don't get it?" Riley was aware that his voice was much higher pitched than usual.

"Well, we don't get much of it."

"What do you mean, man, for Heaven's sake speak plainly."

"Mad Mick's fixed it, the bastard."

"What do you mean he fixed it?" This was unthinkable, this couldn't be true.

"We were acting under orders, on information received," the Sergeant said dully. "We weren't what he calls primarily responsible for the action."

"Then who the bloody hell was?"

"Jane Cabel. She gets three quarters of it. Every bloody penny of seven hundred and fifty pounds."

"And the rest?" said Riley, knowing what the answer would be.

"You and me split that," said the Sergeant: "After they deduct what's owing on our gear."

The sun was hot. The dust hung heavily in the barracks yard Riley could hear the cicadas blaring in the trees as his mind despairingly tried to deduct what he owed the Government from £125.

"Mad Mick said he wants to see you as soon as you show up."

Printed in Great Britain
by Amazon